RIVERDALE SHOWDOWN

The Thompson brothers are held in fear by almost everyone in the small, sleepy community of Riverdale. Brogan McNally's intervention to prevent them bullying a young disabled boy makes the townsfolk realise the Thompsons can be stopped. Then Frank Thompson is killed by Brogan, and the boys' father vows to avenge his son's death. When Brogan and Thompson clash face to face there is an instant understanding and mutual respect although they both know that the final showdown can only mean death for one of them.

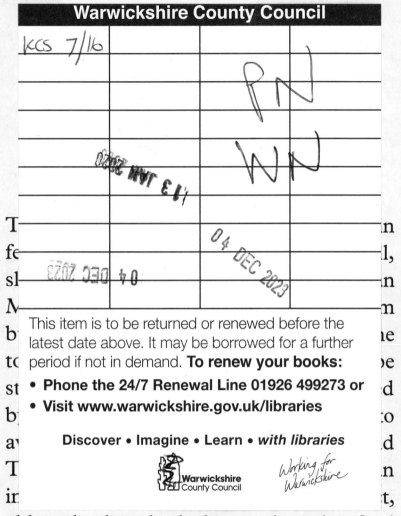
although they both know that the final outcome can only mean death for one of them.

RIVERDALE SHOWDOWN

by
L. D. Tetlow

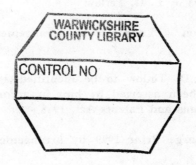

Dales Large Print Books
Long Preston, North Yorkshire,
England.

British Library Cataloguing in Publication Data.

Tetlow, L.D.
  Riverdale showdown.

A catalogue record for this book is
available from the British Library

ISBN 1-85389-951-8 pbk

First published in Great Britain by Robert Hale Ltd., 1998

Cover illustration © Longaron by arrangement with Norma
Editorial S.A.

Published in Large Print 1999 by arrangement with Robert
Hale Ltd.

Dales Large Print is an imprint of
Library Magna Books Ltd.
Printed and bound in Great Britain by
T.J. International Ltd., Cornwall, PL28 8RW.

ONE

Brogan McNally, saddletramp, had seen larger towns and had certainly seen a great many which looked far more prosperous. Riverdale had an air of slow decay and lost grandeur. Some of the houses had obviously once been very elegant but now, with peeling paint, loose boards and chickens strutting in what were once well-kept gardens it was plain that a previously wealthy town had fallen on hard times.

However, there still seemed to be a bustling community and several stores remained open. The town had once supported a bank—now boarded up—and next door—also boarded up—a faded sign proclaimed that an assay office had once occupied the premises. The presence of an assay office told Brogan that previous wealth must have been built up on gold. There had also been at least two saloons along the main street, although now only one remained open and this too gave the impression of having seen better days.

As he rode along the street towards the saloon, three young men suddenly appeared from a nearby alley dragging another young man. All except the young man being dragged were laughing and shouting and one produced a rather ancient looking pistol, told the other two to let the man they were dragging go, which they did, and he immediately began shooting at the man's feet.

'Dance!' he ordered, laughing loudly. 'C'mon, Billy, show everyone how you can dance!'

The young man responded by jumping up and down but what struck Brogan was that he was obviously crippled in some way and, when he stopped jumping when the other young man saw Brogan approaching and briefly lowered his gun, it was apparent that as well as being physically crippled, he was also mentally ill. For a brief moment there was an appealing look at the stranger followed by an inane grin which showed protruding teeth. The young man with the gun looked the new arrival up and down for a moment, laughed and turned his attention back to the cripple and once again ordered him to dance.

'Maybe he don't wanna dance,' said Brogan as he dismounted and tethered his horse to the hitching rail in front of the saloon. He looked about and it was very noticeable that other towns-folk were studiously pretending that they could not see anything.

'What's it got to do with you?' demanded the young man with the gun which he turned towards Brogan.

'Nothin', I guess,' admitted Brogan. 'But even I can see that he's crippled. It just don't seem right to make a cripple dance if he don't want to.'

'Billy don't know no different,' said

one of the others. 'He's daft, allus has been. Folk don't give no heed to daft old Billy.'

The man with the gun looked Brogan up and down again and smiled sarcastically. 'Saddlebum, yeh, I'd say you was a saddlebum. Maybe you can show Billy how it should be done; he don't really dance, he just jumps up an' down.' Immediately he fired a shot at Brogan's feet but Brogan did not even flinch. Suddenly his Colt was in his hand and a single shot sent the young man's gun thudding to the ground. A look of terror mixed with amazement came across his face as slowly he looked down at his hand, now red with blood. Brogan's bullet had seared across the back of his hand just as had been intended. The other two also stared at Brogan in pure disbelief but they made no attempt to go for their guns.

'Let's see if you can dance,' Brogan grinned, as he fired two quick shots into the ground very close to the young man's feet. Instinct rather than the order to dance made him leap backwards and fall over. He stared hatred at the stranger for a few moments and nodded briefly to his companions, a nod which Brogan did not miss and turned his Colt towards them. 'First one to go for his gun is a dead man,' he warned. The other two obviously believed him and held their hands away from their guns. By this time, the previously blind citizens of Riverdale had all miraculously recovered their sight and were beginning to gather round, although not too close. The cripple had moved away from the other three and was now grinning stupidly at his saviour. He stretched out a twisted hand and pointed at Brogan's gun and an unintelligible noise came from his throat. Brogan ignored him, actually feeling rather uncomfortable, and looked about. The young man on the ground picked himself up, looked at his hand and then retrieved his gun.

'You just made the biggest mistake of

your stupid life,' he growled at Brogan. 'Round here nobody tells us Thompsons what to do an' nobody draws a gun on a Thompson an' lives to do it again.'

'I'm still alive,' smiled Brogan.

'Not for long,' growled the young man again. 'My name's Frank Thompson; you'd better remember that name 'cos the next time you either see me or hear my name will be when you die.'

'I'll try to remember it,' grinned Brogan. 'Now I suggest you all go home an' get your ma to dry that wet you've still got behind your ears.' There were threats and abusive language from all three as they trooped across the street where they untethered three horses, mounted and rode swiftly out of town. The other citizens of Riverdale were now talking in small, huddled groups and Brogan had the distinct impression that wagers were being struck as to just how long he would survive. He grinned to himself, reloaded his Colt and returned it to his holster. As he mounted the steps to the saloon, Daft Billy followed him, still grinning inanely. Brogan tried to ignore him.

'You don't come in here!' roared a voice as Brogan, with Daft Billy close behind, entered the saloon. Brogan looked questioningly at the bartender who had barked the order and pointed silently at himself. 'Naw, not you,' said the bartender. 'Daft Billy, he ain't allowed in here, my other customers don't like it. 'Sides, if he gets so much as a smell of liquor inside him he starts pissin' an shittin' all over the place. You're welcome, mister; I'll even give you the first drink on the house—it could be the last free drink you'll ever get. Anyhow, you just brought in a lot of trade I don't normally get this time of the day.' A large number of Riverdale's menfolk were already heading for the saloon just to look at the stranger who had been foolish enough to take on three Thompsons at once and actually survive.

'Thanks,' nodded Brogan, as he leaned

on the bar while the bartender pushed Daft Billy outside. When he returned, Brogan ordered a large beer which he had expected to taste warm and indifferent but found to be cool and refreshing.

'Seems like I just done somethin' almost everyone else in this town wish they had the guts to do,' he said. 'What's so special about these Thompsons?'

'A bunch of murderin' bastards!' grunted the bartender. 'They don't live in town, they've got a tumbledown farm about an hour away up in the hills. There's nine sons and three daughters an' sometimes I wonder just who is the most trouble.'

'Can't your sheriff keep 'em in order?' asked Brogan. By that time the saloon was quite crowded and the bartender was giving out drinks and collecting money. He obviously heard what Brogan had said but was too busy to respond. Brogan waited until everyone had been served and were standing around silently staring at him with just the occasional whisper passing between them. The bartender returned to Brogan and smiled before reaching under the counter and producing a sheriff's star which he threw on the counter in front of Brogan.

'The job's yours if you want it,' he invited. Brogan believed he was serious. 'We ain't had a sheriff for more'n two years. Last one suddenly discovered that he had a very sick relative back East, since then there ain't been nobody who wants the job.'

'Nobody stupid enough, you mean,' said a man standing nearby. 'We even thought about pinnin' the badge on Daft Billy.' He moved forward and stretched out a hand which Brogan chose to ignore. 'Charles Brown,' said the man, introducing himself and then self-consciously lowering the proffered hand and wiping it on his trousers. 'I own the hardware store. I suppose I am what could be loosely called Mayor of Riverdale. Leastwise I'm the only one who seems prepared to do the job.'

'That ain't right, Chas,' said the bartender. 'You know I'd take it on myself but it don't seem right to be mayor an' servin' beer.'

Chas Brown smiled and nodded. 'I saw how you handled yourself out there,' he said to Brogan. 'You were very impressive, plainly a man who is used to handling a gun. May we know your name?'

'McNally, Brogan McNally,' said Brogan. 'An' no, I don't want no job as your sheriff. I tried it once an' it didn't work out. I saw how you handled yourself out there as well,' he continued. 'There wasn't a single one of you who even wanted to help Billy. You was all walkin' about starin' at your feet lookin' for a penny you might have dropped sometime last year.' Chas Brown shuffled uneasily. 'It don't seem much of a town to me what allows someone like Billy to be picked on, even I can see that he's not all there.'

'That's what I've been tellin' 'em ever since he was born,' said a little man pushing forward. 'I'm Billy's grandfather, Silas Morgan. He can't help bein' the way he is. His ma an' pa dumped him on me when they saw how he was an' went off to California somewheres.'

'What do you expect us to do?' asked Chas Brown. 'The town can't be responsible for him.'

'I expect you to do somethin' about them Thompsons,' growled Silas.

'Short of lynchin' them, what can we do?' objected Chas Brown.

'It'd sure solve a problem if you did,' muttered Silas.

'Well, much as I sympathize with your problem,' said Brogan, 'it sure ain't mine. I'm just passin' through. I was kinda hopin' to get a blacksmith to see to my horse, she's got a couple of loose shoes an' if I don't get 'em fixed soon she'll go lame an' it'll be anybody's guess when I get to another blacksmith. I assume you do have one here.'

'My eldest son,' said Silas. 'He helps

me look after Billy. He owns the stable and smithy down by the old church.'

Brogan looked about the room and smiled wryly. 'I reckon he must be just about the only man in town who ain't here. OK, I'll go down an' see him.' He drained his beer, turned and, miraculously, a clear path to the door opened up. He nodded at the bartender and Chas Brown and left the saloon, closely followed by Silas Morgan. Daft Billy grabbed hold of his grandfather's hand as they left and all three made their way towards the old church, Brogan leading his horse. When they arrived, Silas explained what had happened outside the saloon to his son, Walter—a man who certainly did not take after his fragile-looking father. He was tall, almost as tall as Brogan but considerably broader.

'Thanks for that,' Walter said. 'Billy can be a bit of a handful at times, but there's no real harm in him. It's just his appearance what frightens folk. What can

I do for you, Mr McNally?'

'I prefer just plain Brogan,' said Brogan. Walter nodded in acknowledgement. 'My horse has a couple of loose shoes. How much will you charge me to fix 'em?'

'For you, I'll do the job for nothin',' grinned Walter. 'It ain't every day we gets complete strangers doin' anythin' to help Billy. In fact I'll put new shoes all round.' Brogan did not argue, he rarely allowed opportunities like this to pass him by, although he could have paid if he had had to.

He left his horse with Walter and wandered back to the main street, where life had now returned to something like normal. There he found a tiny shop which had a sign outside telling the world that it was 'Madge's Eatin'-House' and that she sold the finest food in town. He was the only customer, which was perhaps as well since the only table was barely large enough for two people. Madge, a woman almost as round as she was tall but quite clean looking, forced herself through a narrow doorway from the kitchen and beamed at him.

'Ain't you the feller what sent them Thompson boys packin'?' she said. 'Pleased to meet you. I'm Madge, Madge Jones. What can I do for you?'

'I was hopin' to get somethin' to eat,' grinned Brogan. 'Your sign outside says this is an eatin'-house.'

'Best you'll ever taste,' she said with a broad smile. 'I got steak, steak pie or you can have ham an' eggs if you want. I don't normally sell ham an' eggs at this time of day though, most folk like them for breakfast.' Brogan looked questioningly around the tiny room, wondering just how many customers she did get. She obviously read his thoughts. 'Hell, this ain't the only room ...' She pushed against what appeared to be a wooden wall which opened up to reveal another dining-room with at least five tables. 'You can eat in here if you'd feel more comfortable,' she

18

invited, 'but I generally only use this front room durin' the day. Most of my trade is early mornin' and evenin'.' Seeing the other room raised the establishment a few points in Brogan's mind.

'Steak,' he said. 'I ain't had me a decent steak in months; mind, steak pie sure sounds good as well.'

'Try the steak now,' she suggested, 'and if you're still around tomorrow, try the steak pie. Vegetables is potatoes, turnips an' turnip greens, oh, and onions if you want.'

'Steak sounds fine to me,' said Brogan. 'With all the trimmin's an' lashings of onions. I love onions.' He looked about again. 'I wouldn't've thought a place like Riverdale would've had enough trade for a place like this.'

'Used to be better,' admitted Madge. 'Even now it ain't too bad, specially at weekends when the farmers all hit town. I gets by.'

'Coffee?' he asked.

'Comin' right up,' she smiled. 'I've got some apple pie, blueberry pie or steamed duff for afters if you want.'

'Coffee, steak with all the trimmin's an' apple pie,' he said, grinning broadly. 'I ain't had me a feast like that in months.'

'One dollar, twenty-five,' she said, holding out her hand. Madge had long since learned to take the money before the customer ate. Brogan dug deep into his pocket and counted out the necessary change.

The meal proved to be as delicious as Madge had claimed it would be and Brogan returned to the smithy feeling pleasantly full. At the smithy he found that his horse had been reshod and that she was at that moment tucking into a meal of bran and oats. She looked up at him as if she were defying him to take her away from her feast. Brogan smiled and left her, but he did remove his rifle from his saddle which was hanging over a partition in the stall.

'I guess it's too late to think about goin' on,' he said to Walter. 'Mind if I spend the night in the stable with my horse?'

'If she don't mind, I don't,' grinned Walter. 'No need to sleep out here though, there's a spare bunk in the room at the back. Nobody uses it these days but the mattress is good an' clean. You can get somethin' to eat at Madge's place ...'

'I've just been there,' said Brogan. 'Last thing I expected to find.'

'She's one hell of a cook,' said Walter. 'She an' my wife are sisters.'

Brogan inspected the room at the back of the stable and decided that it was as good a place as any to spend the night, especially as it appeared to have been offered for free. Actually, although he had had mixed feelings about the town when he had first ridden in, he was beginning to quite like it and since he was in no particular hurry and he certainly had no particular destination, he considered resting up for a couple of days, even if he did have to pay for food and accommodation. He never even considered the possible threat posed by the Thompsons.

However, that threat was raised when he went into the hardware store to buy some bullets and a new billycan—his old one had developed a leak. Chas Brown looked up as if surprised that he had not yet been killed. 'Glad to see you're still alive,' he greeted. 'What can I get you or have you come to tell me you've changed your mind and want to take the sheriff's job?'

'I ain't changed my mind,' said Brogan. 'I was goin' to buy a box of bullets an' a billycan, but it looks like I'll be wastin' my money if you think I won't live to use either of 'em.'

'Didn't mean it to sound like that,' said Chas, suddenly realizing that he might be turning away a sale. He glanced at Brogan's Colt and rifle with something of an expert eye and reached for a box of fifty bullets on a shelf. 'One box?' he said, hoping for a further sale. Brogan nodded, both rifle and Colt used the same ammunition, it saved a lot of problems. A billycan was produced from behind a pile of cooking pots and he enquired if other utensils were needed. Brogan again shook his head. 'That'll be five dollars exactly,' he said.

'Five dollars!' said Brogan. 'How much is the billycan?'

'Fifty cents,' replied Chas. 'The ammunition is four fifty.'

'I only paid three dollars a box in Boulder City,' objected Brogan.

'This ain't Boulder City,' Chas correctly pointed out. 'If you want to go back there and buy some, be my guest. I'd say it was no more'n two weeks ridin'. Four dollars fifty cents is the price out here and I ain't loadin' the price just because you're passing through. Four fifty is the regular price.'

Brogan realized that he had little choice but to agree. He did have a few bullets but he always liked to have more in hand. He did not use that many but he never liked to be caught short. He paid Chas Brown and returned to the stable to put his purchases in his bags when he was aware of being watched. He turned to see a tall, thin, weaselly featured man staring at him.

'Want somethin'?' he asked.

'Just lookin',' drawled the man, his thumbs hooked meaningfully into the top of his gunbelt.

'Ain't no law against that I suppose,' nodded Brogan. 'What's so interestin'?'

'Just lookin' at the man who was foolish enough to take on the Thompsons,' the man drawled again. 'My name's Jimmy Thompson, it was my son you shot.'

'Mister Thompson,' sighed Brogan, sensing that Jimmy Thompson was not, at that moment, intent on pushing matters too far. 'If I had intended to kill your son he would've been dead now. I aimed for his hand and that's what I hit. You can tell him he has to learn a thing or two yet.'

'He's just like all young folk,' said Thompson with the hint of a smile, 'think they know it all an' us old folk don't know nothin'. He's right about one thing though, you look an' smell like a saddletramp.'

'You don't exactly smell like a rose,' said Brogan, pointedly sniffing the air. Thompson smiled but did not seem to take offence.

'I thought I'd make this a friendly visit,' said Thompson. 'Since you is a stranger in town an' don't know who's in charge around here. I'm givin' you the chance to get the hell out while you can. There ain't been no damage done to nobody—yet. Only thing what has been hurt is my son's pride but it won't do him any harm to get a bit of experience behind him. Take my advice, Mr Saddlebum, get out of town right now. If you is still here this evenin' or tomorrow, I can't be held responsible for what happens to you. In fact I might even have to kill you myself. It wouldn't be nothin' personal you understand, just a matter of family pride.'

'I'm glad it wouldn't be personal,' said Brogan, sarcastically. 'I hope you don't mind if I have to kill you or your son, it wouldn't be nothin' personal either.'

Thompson nodded and slowly turned to leave. 'Don't say I didn't warn you,' he said, looking back. 'Frank has vowed to kill you and while I think he's a bit too much of a greenhorn to be takin' on a man like you, there ain't nothin' I can do to talk him out of it. If you do kill him, you'd better know that I ain't no greenhorn. You have the look of a man who ain't easily scared off an' I reckon you know how to handle yourself an' that gun. It'd be interestin' to see who is faster, you or me.'

Brogan had the distinct feeling that that was no idle boast, but if there was one thing that was guaranteed to make him dig his heels in, it was being told to leave somewhere. Whereas before he had only been considering staying a few days, he was now determined to do so.

'Yeah, I saw him,' said Walter Morgan when Brogan told him of the visitor. 'I deliberately stayed out of the way. I ain't no gunman but Jimmy had a hell of a reputation in his younger days an' I hear that he can still outshoot almost everyone. I don't know how you are with your gun, but I'd take his advice and get the hell out of town right now. Of all the Thompsons he's the only one who says what he means an' means what he says.'

'My horse needs a few days' rest,' said Brogan. This further piece of advice to leave had simply reinforced his determination to stay. 'Maybe you'd better tell your undertaker to measure up a few boxes.'

Walter shook his head. 'Mister, I don't understand men like you. It's almost as if you have a death wish. This ain't your town, you don't owe it or anyone in it nothin' so why the hell risk your life just because of some stupid pride?'

Actually Walter was talking perfect sense and Brogan knew it. It was nothing more than stubborn pride which was making him stay and it was stubborn pride which would one day kill him. Nevertheless, his pride almost always triumphed over logic and this occasion was not going to be an exception. He left the stable and decided that if he was going to die, he might as well die with a stomach full of good food and at that moment the call of Madge's steak pie, potatoes, turnips and turnip greens followed by either apple or blueberry pie was too strong to resist.

TWO

Since he had nothing better to do, that evening found Brogan propping up the counter in the saloon toying with a glass of beer. There were about twenty other occupants all of whom seemed rather surprised that he was still around. The general consensus had been that he would not dare risk incurring the wrath of the Thompsons, however the initial surprise eventually waned and most of them turned their attention to the far more important matter of playing cards.

'Have you thought about the offer of the sheriff's job?' asked the bartender. 'We could pay five dollars a week plus board. The office needs some work done on it, but we would see to that. There's a good room at the back or maybe we could find you a house if you wanted.'

'Don't need to think about it,' said Brogan. 'That kind of job ain't for me. I tried it once. In fact no job an' no one place is for me. The only place I'm likely to take up permanent residence is a cemetery if I'm lucky. Otherwise it's likely to just be a hole in the ground in the desert or end up bein' buzzard meat. Whatever happens I won't be takin' much interest in it. I'm too old to think about changin' now; I've been travellin' almost all my life an' I guess I just need to keep on the move either until I drop dead or a bullet finishes me off.'

'Then why ain't you moved on?' smiled the bartender. 'The Thompsons ain't folk to be passed off lightly. Once they've set their mind on doin' somethin' they do it, as a good many have found to their cost. Most of 'em are now in permanent residence in the cemetery.'

'Maybe thats's 'cos once I've set my mind on somethin' I do it,' Brogan grinned. 'I guess you could call me stubborn or mule-headed, but one thing I don't like is a bunch of no-goods tellin' me what to do. Anyhow, I've been travellin' for almost two weeks an' both me an' my horse need the rest.'

'You could be in for a longer rest than you bargained for,' said the bartender, whose name was Mick Fletcher.

'I've survived so far,' said Brogan,

dismissively. Mick shrugged and went to serve another customer.

Ten minutes later Silas Morgan came in, panting for breath. He looked around and saw Brogan and went up to him. 'The Thompsons are on their way,' he wheezed. 'At least three of them are, young Frank, Wilbur and Carl. Carl's the one you have to watch, he's the eldest of the sons an' he's real mean an' no slouch when it comes to usin' a gun.'

'It's a free country, so they tell me,' nodded Brogan.

'Just thought you ought to know,' gasped Silas. 'They should be here in a few minutes.'

The message had been overheard by a group at a nearby table who all looked apprehensively at each other and decided that they had had enough of playing cards and left. On their way out they told others that the Thompsons were coming. One or two more suddenly realized that it was time they went home but the remainder, ten of them, opted to stay and see what happened, although they all moved tables to be closer to the door just in case they had to make a quick exit. Five minutes later the swing doors burst open and three men walked in. Frank was the only one whom Brogan recognized but he deliberately did not look at them; instead he studied their reflection in the big mirror behind the bar, but he was ready for action.

The three men marched up to the bar and leant across it a few feet away from Brogan and ordered three beers. 'The saddlebum is payin',' said Frank, his hand bandaged as a result of his earlier clash with Brogan. Mick Fletcher glanced at Brogan.

'Saddlebums don't run to that kind of money,' said Brogan. 'Anyhow, I don't believe in encouragin' youngsters to drink.'

'Did you hear somethin'?' Frank said to his companions.

'I thought I did but I didn't quite catch

it,' said Carl, a big man with several teeth missing which Brogan assumed he had lost in a fight. 'Can you smell somethin'?' he asked the others. 'Have either of you trodden in any dog shit on the way in?' They all examined the soles of their boots very pointedly and shook their heads. 'Well there sure is somethin' that stinks pretty rotten in here,' he continued. 'Mick,' he said to the bartender, 'you ain't let Daft Billy in an' let him drink dregs an' shit all over the place like he usually does?' Mick chose to ignore them and busied himself cleaning some glasses. Carl leant forward slightly and looked at Brogan. 'I reckon I know where the smell's comin' from,' he laughed. Brogan too chose to ignore them. The one thing he had learned over many years was not to rise to comments about his personal hygiene or looks. 'Mick's waitin' for you to pay for these drinks,' continued Carl.

'You pay for your own,' said Mick. 'You know the rules: you don't pay you don't get served again.' The three of them laughed and Frank produced a coin and threw it on to the counter, Mick picked it up and gave him some change.

'Maybe you should have a rule keepin' stinkin' saddlebums out,' said Wilbur. 'It's gettin' so's decent folk can't get a drink without bein' stunk out.'

'How would you know what decent folk think,' said Brogan. He realized that he might have been better off ignoring them, but he could not resist goading them.

'Did you say somethin'?' Wilbur asked Frank. 'I thought I heard someone speak. Maybe I was just hearin' things.'

'I heard it too,' said Carl. 'I think the noise came from that pile of shit against the bar. Hey, turd,' he said to Brogan. 'Did you say somethin'?'

Mick Fletcher put down a glass and spread his arms meaningfully across the counter and stared at them. 'OK, you had your fun, now drink up an' get out of here. You might be able to scare most folk in this town but there are one or two of us you don't.'

'We got some unfinished business,' said Carl, easing himself away from the counter and nodding to the other two. Immediately there was a scrape of chairs on the wooden floor as two more customers suddenly realized that it was past their bedtime and left. The three of them stood behind Brogan, Carl in the middle, but Brogan had been ready for just this, he had fully expected it and it certainly was not the first time it had happened to him. He glanced in the mirror and smiled.

He had long since learned that to apparently ignore people like them tended to make them very annoyed and in his experience men who were annoyed were prone to make mistakes and he did not think they would be an exception. He was quite right, their reflections in the mirror showed that they were becoming agitated.

'Hey, saddlebum!' grated Carl. 'We is talkin' to you.'

Very slowly Brogan turned his head and stared at them. 'Sorry, I wasn't listenin',' he said. 'I don't normally listen to kids prattlin', it never seems to make any sense. What was it you wanted?' His apparent complete lack of interest and calmness seemed to unnerve the three of them and they glanced at each other, Carl licking his lips with the tip of his tongue. 'It's gettin' late,' added Brogan; 'Ain't it about time you was all tucked up in your beds where all good boys should be?'

'Funny feller!' grated Carl. 'I hear you're pretty handy with that gun of yours but I reckon you just got lucky this mornin'.'

'Could be,' agreed Brogan, turning his attention to his beer. This seemed to annoy Carl even more.

Brogan heard the three of them take a couple of steps backwards and at the same time two other customers decided that it was an opportune moment to leave. His keen hearing also heard the very faint scrape of metal against leather as Carl's hand went to his gun.

'Bastard!' hissed Carl. 'Now you die!' However, he was too late as Brogan suddenly turned ...

Carl Thompson had hardly pulled his gun out of his holster as a single bullet from Brogan's Colt thudded into his chest. For a brief moment he remained perfectly still but then rasped slightly as his knees buckled beneath him. The other two stared in total disbelief at their brother as he fell and then jerked their heads to look at the saddletramp as he spoke.

'Either of you fancy joinin' him?' he asked. 'It can be arranged, just go for them guns of yours, that's all you have to do.'

'Carl!' croaked Wilbur. 'You've killed Carl ...'

'Very observant of you,' nodded Brogan. However, a moan from the floor indicated that Carl was not yet dead. 'Looks like he might've got lucky,' continued Brogan. 'I reckon you'd best get a doctor to him pretty damned fast.'

'Go get Doc Graham,' Mick Fletcher ordered one of the men standing at the door. The man gulped, nodded and disappeared. 'That was some fancy move,' Mick said to Brogan as he came round the counter and looked down at Carl Thompson. 'Self-defence of course, I can vouch for that, I saw everythin' an' there were other witnesses.' He looked at the men still at the tables by the door. 'I guess you can all vouch for that.'

'Didn't see nothin',' croaked one of the men. 'I was drinkin' at the time, I didn't see a thing.' The others agreed with him and all decided that they had better not hang around any longer just in case they would be expected to explain things to someone, especially any of the Thompsons.

'Nobody ever sees a damned thing,' sighed Mick. 'I guess it don't matter though, there sure ain't nobody here goin' to arrest you for it even if they wanted to, they'd be too scared someone might expect them to take on the job of sheriff.'

Frank and Wilbur Thompson were kneeling beside their brother, Frank wiping a trickle of blood from the corner of Carl's mouth. He looked up at Brogan with hatred-filled eyes. 'OK, so you're fast an' good with that gun an' maybe we underestimated you, but us Thompsons learn fast an' I can assure you none of us is goin' to make the same mistake twice ...'

'You just did,' Brogan pointed out. 'You should've learned from what happened earlier.'

'Yeh ... well, I did warn Carl but I gotta admit that he's a bit bone-headed about things like that. I can tell you this though, Mr Saddlebum, your days are certainly numbered an' maybe your time on this earth can be reckoned in hours when pa hears about this. Our pa sure ain't a man to be frightend of a saddlebum or to let him get the better of him.'

'I've already met your pa,' said Brogan.

'He don't strike me as a man who rushes into things. Maybe you could learn a thing or two from him, but I guess you ain't no different from all young men, you think us older folk don't know nothin'. I was probably just the same myself when I was your age.' From what he had seen and heard of the Thompsons so far, Brogan knew that the older man, their father, was far more dangerous than any of the others. Jimmy Thompson had had the look of a cold, calculating and very experienced man, making him much more of a threat than any of his hot-headed sons.

Doc Graham, a surprisingly old man whom Brogan discovered had arrived when the gold was at its height but was now too old to consider leaving, panted into the room and pushed Frank and Wilbur to one side and then ripped open Carl's shirt and peered at the wound. Carl was unconscious but still breathing and, after listening to his chest for a while, the doc stood up.

'Nothin' I can do for him here,' he said. 'Bring him over to my office, I have to get that bullet out.'

'Will he live?' asked Wilbur.

'It looks to me like the bullet hasn't done any damage to any vital part of his heart, but I can't tell for sure until I get inside his chest. I reckon he'll live but he'll be mighty sore for a few weeks.'

'In more ways than one,' growled Frank. 'C'mon, Wilbur, let's do what the doc says an' get him to the office.'

'Be careful with him,' warned Doc Graham. 'You'd best make some sort of stretcher to carry him on, carrying or dragging him round could finish off the job the bullet hasn't.'

'How do we do that?' asked Frank.

'You need a couple of poles,' said Brogan. 'Take your jackets off an' thread the poles through the buttoned up jackets, that should hold him.'

'I've got a couple of poles out the back,' said Mick Fletcher. He ran outside and returned with the poles. Frank and Wilbur took off their jackets and, very strangely, accepted Brogan's guidance and threaded the poles through and then eased Carl on to the makeshift stretcher.

By that time it appeared that the entire population of Riverdale, including women and children, had arrived outside the saloon as if expecting to see a lot of blood and gore, but they were disappointed. Loud whispers rippled round as the injured man was brought out and, when Brogan appeared, it seemed that they all took one step backwards. When the crowd had seen Carl Thompson taken into the doctor's office, they broke up into small groups and once again Brogan had the feeling that wagers on his survival were being laid, only this time the odds were considerably shorter. Charles Brown, the hardware store owner and town mayor followed Brogan and Mick Fletcher back into the saloon.

'I fear the worst,' he moaned. 'It was bad enough you shootin' that gun out of Frank's hand, but to shoot Carl was just about the worst thing you could've done.'

'From whose point of view?' Brogan asked, smiling sardonically. 'Maybe you would have preferred it if I had been killed. I suppose it wouldn't have mattered, after all, who cares about a saddletramp? Accordin' to young Frank I am already a dead man so no matter what I do can't make matters any the worse for me.'

Chas Brown gulped and glanced at Mick. 'I am afraid that the Thompsons will take it out on us as well,' he said. 'There's nine of them remember.'

Brogan laughed. 'Nine, is that all?' he sneered. 'How many people are there in this town? Two hundred, three hundred?'

'You don't seem to understand, Mr McNally,' flustered the mayor. 'The folk of Riverdale are not gunmen. Most of them have hardly ever handled anything other than scatterguns ...'

'I've seen many a man blasted by one of those,' said Brogan. 'They can kill a man just as easy as anythin' else. Don't tell me folk won't stand up for themselves if they have to. That's what men like the Thompsons trade on, the fact that folk like you are too scared to do anythin' an' just lie down to be trampled on. Still, if that's the way you want it I guess that's what you'll get.'

'We are not killers,' objected Chas. 'That's why we need someone like you to take on the job of sheriff.'

'And I am a killer!' grated Brogan. 'Mr Brown, that's just where you're wrong. Just 'cos I ain't afraid to shoot a man don't turn me into no killer.'

'I ... didn't mean to imply that you were, Mr McNally ...' Brogan did not normally like being called McNally, but in this case he thought it was more appropriate and did not correct the mayor. 'But you have just made the point yourself,' said Chas, 'you are not afraid to kill if necessary and you have shown that you are not easily frightened.'

'Forget it,' said Brogan, turning his attention back to his unfinished beer. 'I move on when I'm ready which is goin' to be pretty damned soon. After that what happens between you an' the Thompsons is your problem, not mine. All I can say is get yourselves together, stand up to 'em an' you'll find that they'll soon accept the situation. Folk like that usually do.'

'We still need a sheriff,' said Chas. 'Ain't that right, Mick?' he said to the bartender.

'Sure do,' agreed Mick, 'but McNally's right, it's our problem, not his. Even if he did take on the job, we all know that it would only be for a short while, after that we would have to get someone permanent.'

'But we need someone to sort out the Thompsons,' said Chas.

'That's just about the size of it,' laughed Brogan. 'A saddletramp like me won't be missed if somethin' goes wrong an' he gets killed. If he succeeds, he rids you of a problem, so either way, you can't really lose. You'd better pin that badge on Daft Billy, he's just about the only man I know who'd be daft enough to take it on those terms.'

Chas Brown made some noises about things not being like that but by that time Brogan was not listening and Chas left. Brogan had another beer, this time on the house by which time the curious and the ghoulish had drifted back into the saloon and were either standing around gawping at Brogan or were huddled in small groups discussing what they considered to be his very limited future. The place was becoming too crowded and too stuffy for Brogan's liking and he went out into the street and took a deep breath of fresh air.

He thought about going to Doc Graham's office to see how Carl Thompson was progressing, but decided that the

Thompsons were not his problem and that it was almost time that he was in his bed anyway. The fact that Frank and Wilbur Thompson were still in town, probably at the doc's office, was obvious from the fact that three horses were still tethered outside the saloon. Brogan knew that they belonged to the Thompsons simply because he had not yet seen anyone else in town with a horse. A few minutes after settling himself for the night, Brogan heard the muffled sound of horses' hooves along the street. He listened as the sounds slowly faded before he closed his eyes, a smile playing on his face.

'He'll be OK,' grunted Doc Graham as his blood-covered hands took the bullet from the pair of long tweezers and glanced briefly at it before dropping it into a basket. He peered into the hole in Carl's chest once more, inserted a finger and probed around, making both Frank and Wilbur feel quite ill. 'No real damage done,' continued the doc, 'he's a strong boy and this shouldn't cause him much bother.' He took hold of a curved needle which had been threaded with gut and proceeded to sew up the hole. This was too much for Frank and he was forced to leave the room. Doc Graham glanced at him as he left and nodded. 'It's surprising just how many men who will kill anyone or beat them to a pulp can't stand the sight of someone being sewn up. Anyhow,' he said to Wilbur, 'don't let him do anything too hard for a couple of weeks at least, the shock could kill him.'

'Can he stay here for the night?' asked Wilbur. 'There ain't no way we can get him home at this time of night. We'll come with a buggy or the buckboard tomorrow.'

'This ain't no hospital,' muttered Doc Graham, 'but I guess you're right. OK, but make sure you're here early in the morning. You can tell your pa that my fee for this little lot is five dollars and that I want cash, not payment in kind.'

Wilbur nodded and went to join his brother who immediately dragged him into the shadow of the doorway and nodded along the street. 'We get him while he's asleep!' whispered Frank. 'We pretend to ride out of town, but we only go as far as the river. Gettin' into the stable should be easy enough. Pa did say he thought that was where he was dossin'; in the back room he reckons. Have you got your knife with you?' Wilbur produced a bowie knife. 'Good,' continued Frank. 'Let's go. We give him time to get to sleep, say about an hour. We don't use guns, that'd attract too much attention.'

'You scared?' asked Wilbur.

'You oughta know better'n that,' hissed Frank. 'It'd just be better if folk didn't know he was dead until the mornin'.'

They took their horses, leading Carl's, and slowly headed out of town, making a slight diversion to make sure that the saddletramp heard them go.

Although Frank and Wilbur were very quiet, they were not quiet enough for Brogan not to detect them. The first thing that alerted Brogan to their presence was the slight but sudden blast of cold wind into the stables as the door was opened. Even the little bit it was opened was enough to cause the wind to brush across Brogan's face and years of conditioning had taught him to react to such things.

On the face of it though, there was no reaction at all from Brogan; he hardly moved a muscle but his eyes penetrated the darkness, using what little light there was and his ears picked up even the slightest sound of straw crushing beneath leather boots. At the same time his hand tightened slightly around the handle of his gun and he waited ...

Frank led the way, feeling the wall round towards the back room with Wilbur close behind. Both men knew the layout of the stable very well, having been there many times in the past. They eventually came to the room and very slowly eased down the catch, taking great care not to make too much noise and then they eased the door inwards and slipped into the room.

There was just about enough moonlight from the small window to allow them to make out the sleeping form on the bed. Frank touched his brother's arm and pointed. Both men stepped forward and the knives in their hands struck into the body. They had stabbed him at least three times each when Wilbur suddenly ripped aside the blankets and felt the body.

'Bloody straw!' he hissed. 'We been had, Frank, we've been tryin' to kill a pile of straw.'

A laugh from somewhere in the stable made them both decide to leave as fast as they could. They reached the door after falling several times, spurred on by the unseen presence of the saddletramp. Brogan's laughter seemed to be on top of them as they forced open the door and ran as fast as they could for the safety of the river, where they had left their horses. They even imagined that the saddletramp was running after them. They rode off as fast as they could, arriving home at just after midnight but not daring to tell their father about their failed attempt to stab the saddletramp in his bed. His reaction to the news about his son, Carl, was bad enough as he swore and cursed their ineptness.

THREE

Brogan was in Madge's Eatin'-House enjoying a large breakfast of ham, three eggs and a mug of coffee. He had been rather surprised at the number of customers there were, at least twelve who had either already been there or came in afterwards, and the signs were that there were more to follow. He had just finished when the Thompsons, headed by the father, Jimmy Thompson, rode into town. They had a buckboard on which to transport Carl back to their farm. Brogan idly watched them through the window as four of them went into Doc Graham's office and he wondered if matters were going to be left at that or whether any of them intended carrying out their threat to try to kill him. After a time, when Carl was on the buckboard, it appeared that there was something of an argument going on between the sons and their father, but it seemed that the old man finally won and all except him left town. Jimmy Thompson went into one of the stores and Brogan finished his breakfast, sensing that he was about to see more of the elder Thompson. He wandered slowly back to the stable where Walter had started work and who looked up as Brogan entered.

'They've taken Carl back,' announced Walter. 'I hear he's goin' to be OK, but

I don't think it will make things any easier for you.'

'I saw 'em,' nodded Brogan. 'The old man stayed behind an' I don't think it was 'cos he had other business in town.'

Walter smiled slightly and nodded. 'Jimmy is a different matter to his sons,' he said. 'In his younger days he had a hell of a reputation of being mighty handy with a gun and I don't think he's a man who is easily scared. Watch him, Brogan, he might seem a bit slow but I can assure you he's more dangerous than a rattlesnake.'

'I already worked that out,' agreed Brogan. 'Don't worry, I won't start anythin'; as far as I'm concerned it's up to him to make the first move.'

Brogan was combing his horse when he sensed rather than heard someone behind him and he needed no second guess as to exactly who that someone was. He did not even turn to look but continued combing the horse.

'You could've been dead,' said a voice.

'It ain't often a man presents such an easy target. You're either very foolish or very sure of yourself, McNally. Personally I'd say it was because you're very sure of yourself.'

'Mister Thompson,' said Brogan, still not turning to face the man. 'I got ears that can detect a fly landin' on a piece of shit from a hundred yards. I knew you were there an' I can assure you, you would've been just as dead. What can I do for you?'

'Nothin',' said Thompson. 'I'm just lookin'. I was right about you, you ain't a man to be tangled with, especially by hotheads like my boys. I believe you, I reckon you did know I was here. From what I hear that was some mighty fast work by you in the saloon. Did you aim to kill Carl?'

'Sure did,' said Brogan honestly, this time turning to face Thompson. 'I must be gettin' old, your boy should've been on his way to the cemetery instead of bein' taken home.'

'I can respect a man who gives an honest answer,' nodded Thompson. 'The doc says Carl will be OK, he's just got to take it easy for a while. Maybe I should thank you, he always was a bit of a hothead, maybe this'll teach him that he ain't the best.'

'From what I hear, he can't be,' said Brogan. 'I hear that you are pretty good when it comes to things like that.'

'There wasn't anyone better in my day,' smiled Thompson. 'Like you though, I'm gettin' older an' I don't take the risks like I used to, but I reckon I can still give a pretty good account of myself. I was just wonderin' how things would be between you an' me. You intrigue me, McNally, I hear you've been a saddlebum all your life but you're the first one I've ever met who ain't got a great big yeller streak runnin' down his back.'

'Just goes to show that we ain't all the same,' said Brogan. 'An' I ain't never stole nothin' off nobody an' I ain't never raped a woman an' I ain't never killed a man who didn't ask for it. I guess I must be one of a rare breed, an honest saddletramp.'

Jimmy Thompson shrugged his shoulders. 'It's a pity you ain't like other saddlebums, it'd make killin' you that much easier. As things stand I even feel quite sad at the thought of either me or one of my boys killin' you, but that's what's goin' to happen, McNally. If I let you get away with this it might just make some other folk in this town think that maybe us Thompsons ain't so scary after all.'

'An' that's important to you,' said Brogan, 'bein' able to put the fear of Christ into everyone?'

'It goes back a long way,' said Thompson, 'Somethin' of a feud between the Thompsons an' the town of Riverdale, but that ain't your concern. All I can say is the only chance you've got is to saddle that horse of yours an' get the hell out of this place as fast as possible, but even that wouldn't guarantee your survival.'

'We could settle the matter here an' now if you want,' said Brogan, straightening himself a little and squaring up to Thompson. Jimmy Thompson smiled wryly and shook his head.

'You'd like that, wouldn't you?' he said. 'Just you an' me. Sure, I've even given the matter some thought myself an' I can assure you that if I was a year or two younger I might've taken you up on it. I guess you could say I am an honest man too, McNally, but at least I'm honest enough to know that my chances of beatin' you in any shoot out are not all that good. These days I like the odds more in my favour.'

'An' you've got eight sons to do your dirty work for you.'

'Seven,' corrected Thompson. 'Carl ain't goin' to be no use for a few weeks. But I've got three daughters too an' they can be real hell-cats if they want to be. My old lady ain't scared to tackle anyone, either.'

'OK,' shrugged Brogan. 'So includin' you, the odds against me are twelve to one. I've been up against worse odds than that an' I'm still here.'

'I can believe that,' nodded Thompson. 'I knew from the start that you was somethin' different an' in another age I reckon you an' me would've made a great team.'

'That's where you're wrong, Mr Thompson,' said Brogan with a slight laugh. 'I'm a loner, allus have been an' allus will be.'

'I guess so,' agreed Thompson giving another shrug. 'I was just the same; I didn't like bein' beholden to nobody either, but don't say I didn't warn you, that's all.'

'I'll think about that when I'm dead,' said Brogan. 'We all gotta die sometime an' I suppose this just could be my time. By the way, your other two boys, Frank an' Wilbur, they left somethin' behind last night.'

'Last night?' queried Thompson.

'Yeah, I guess they didn't tell you,' smiled Brogan. 'It seems they decided to pay me a visit before they went home.' He produced a bowie knife and tossed it to Thompson. 'I don't know which one it belongs to, but they left it behind when they ran off last night after tryin' to stab me in bed. Only thing was, they killed a pile of straw instead.'

Jimmy Thompson picked up the knife and laughed. 'Frank's,' he said. 'Wilbur's knife ain't like this. So, the idiots thought they could kill you while you was asleep an' they fell for that old trick. You had your chance to kill them then an' even I would've said it was their own stupid fault, so why didn't you?'

'I don't kill nobody unless I have to,' said Brogan, 'especially not kids still wet behind the ears like them two. They ran off like they'd come up against a bear or somethin'.'

'Wet behind the ears they might be,' said

Thompson, 'but they is still Thompsons an' still dangerous.'

'To themselves maybe,' said Brogan. 'OK, Mister Thompson,' he continued, 'unless you want to take up my offer of a showdown, I got me other things to do.'

'Oh, there'll be a showdown all right,' assured Thompson. 'The odds will be all in my favour though. Just make sure those eyes up your arse are workin', that's all.'

'They will be,' said Brogan.

Jimmy Thompson turned and disappeared up the street leaving Brogan to wonder just what might have happened had Jimmy Thompson taken up the offer of a shoot out. One thing was quite certain: despite Thompson saying that he liked the odds more in his favour, he was not a man Brogan would normally choose to set himself up against.

'Now that's the first time I've ever seen or heard him give any respect to any man,' said Walter Morgan, who had overheard everything. 'Normally he wouldn't hesitate, he'd've blasted whoever it was into the next life. You must have somethin' that scares him.'

'I ain't scared of him,' said Brogan. 'That's what frightens him. He's used to havin' his own way an' it kinda throws him off balance when someone stands up to him. I ain't scared of him but I must admit that I do have a healthy respect for him, not so much as who he is but what he is. He's just about the first man I've come up against who's like me in many ways. I know I challenged him but in a way I'm mighty glad he turned me down. Most men I can judge pretty well, even to how fast they might be with a gun, an' he's one of the few who I think might just get the better of me, but don't tell him that.'

'How much longer are you hangin' around?' asked Walter.

'I was thinkin' about leavin' tomorrow,' said Brogan. 'There don't seem much cause to hang about.'

'More cause not to hang about,' said Walter. 'Don't worry about us, I reckon we can handle the Thompsons if we have to.'

'Maybe!' grinned Brogan. 'You don't seem to have handled 'em too well so far so I can't see you bein' much different now.'

'I meant we can put up with 'em,' said Walter. 'Normally they ain't much more bother than a boil on the back of the neck.'

'You can lance a boil,' Brogan pointed out.

Some time later, Brogan was wandering down the street, having just been to the general store to buy a few supplies he needed, when he was approached by Chas Brown.

'Have you reconsidered the sheriff's job?' asked Chas. 'We've been talkin' about it an' we can increase the salary to seven dollars a week, all found, with meals at Madge's an' as much ammunition as you want.'

'If anythin' was goin' to swing it,' laughed Brogan, 'it'd be the food at Madge's. Sorry, Mister Brown, no deal. I'll be on my way tomorrow.'

'I wouldn't be too sure about that,' said Chas. 'I've just seen four of the Thompsons ride into town.'

'They've got a right to, I guess,' said Brogan. 'Would it make any difference if I was wearin' a sheriff's star?'

'Probably not,' admitted Chas. 'The whole town knows that Jimmy Thompson went to see you this mornin' an' that nothin' happened. That's the kind of thing that makes me think you bein' sheriff would be good for the town. If you had been any other man we would've been diggin' your grave right now. Everyone is wonderin' just why Jimmy hasn't killed you yet.'

'I thought you said me bein' sheriff wouldn't make no difference?' said Brogan.

'I think they would still try to kill you,' said Chas.

'So this way they still kill me,' smiled Brogan. 'It seems I'm dead whether I'm a sheriff or not an' you could offer me seven hundred dollars a week if you wanted to. If I'm not around to spend it, there's not a lot of difference between seven and seven hundred.'

'I must say you are taking the whole thing very calmly,' said Chas. 'Other men would have left town long ago.'

'I ain't other men!' said Brogan, rather boastfully.

After he had taken his purchases back to the stable and put them in his saddle-bags, more out of sheer pig-headedness than anything else, Brogan deliberately chose to find the four Thompsons. The logical place to start seemed to be the saloon and he was not disappointed, the four of them were sitting round a table playing cards. There had been other customers in the saloon when the Thompsons had entered, but one minute later they had the place to themselves, apart from Mick Fletcher.

When Brogan came into the room, they laid down their cards and glanced at each other. Brogan's hand deliberately but briefly flicked the handle of his Colt for them to see. He went to the bar and ordered a beer, his back towards them but ready for action.

'I recognize two of 'em,' he said to Mick, keeping his voice low. 'Frank an' Wilbur, who're the other two?'

'Amos an' Johnny,' replied Mick. 'They ain't up to much, they just do what they're told, but they ain't afraid to kill a man, in fact Amos has.'

Brogan turned and smiled at the four sardonically. 'Hi, there,' he said. 'Glad to hear that your brother is goin' to pull through, although by rights he should've been dead, still some folk just get lucky I guess. Frank, I gave your pa a knife you dropped in the stable last night, did he give it back to you? It was very careless of you to leave it lyin' around.'

'Very funny!' hissed Frank. 'Sure, he

gave it back an' he also gave me a black eye for not killin' you.' He turned his head to show Brogan a bruised eye. 'You think you're very clever but no saddlebum could ever be clever enough to get the better of any Thompson.'

'I make it three times I've got the better of you,' grinned Brogan. 'How's the hand? Maybe you an' Wilbur should stick to murderin' bales of straw.' He looked at Amos and Johnny. 'Have they told you about that? Last night they murdered a bundle of straw. I'd say that was just about their standard.' There was a slight movement from Wilbur, who had his hands beneath the table. Immediately Brogan's Colt was in his hand, levelled at them. 'I wouldn't even think about it if I was you,' he continued. 'Put your hands flat on the table, all of you,' he ordered. 'Wilbur, put that gun of yours on the table too, I get kinda nervous when I can't see people's hands.' Three of them slowly placed their hands on the table and Wilbur also placed his gun down. Brogan looked at the gun and smiled. 'A five-shot Adams,' he said. 'I ain't seen one of them in a long time. Trouble with them is they don't have the range an' ain't so accurate.'

'Accurate enough to kill any saddlebum,' growled Wilbur.

'Maybe it's as well that the feller usin' it ain't so accurate,' said Brogan. 'You should get your pa to teach you a thing or two.' He looked at Mick. 'Do you want 'em to leave?'

'Naw, they can stay, as long as they pay their way. Their money is just as good as anyone else's,' he replied.

'Have it your way,' nodded Brogan. 'Say thank you to the nice man,' he said. They just scowled at him in response. 'Now, I've got me other things to do. Don't drink too much beer, youngsters like you can't take it.' He returned his Colt to his holster and went towards the door. Suddenly he was twisting round and at the same time dropping to one knee, his Colt seemingly miraculously back in his hand. There were no shots but Wilbur had his gun in his hand aimed in Brogan's general direction. 'Son,' said Brogan, 'from this distance I ain't never been known to miss. When will any of you learn? Now, put that gun down real slow, I'm gettin' kinda nervous an' when I'm nervous I tend to shoot people.' Wilbur placed the gun on the table again and scowled. Brogan stood up and laughed and slowly but deliberately replaced his gun. 'That's four times?' he said.

A large crowd had gathered outside the saloon almost as soon as Brogan had gone in and four men had been peering through the window, keeping up a running commentary on what was happening. When Brogan had turned and dropped to one knee, the watchers had suddenly either flattened themselves on the boardwalk or had fled. The reason was quite simple: they had been in the firing line.

As he emerged, the crowd seemed to take one step backwards, as they had before and he heard one mother warning her obviously wayward son that if he did not behave himself, the dirty old saddletramp would come and take him away. Brogan pulled a face at another child who was aiming a wooden gun at him and the child immediately screamed and hid himself behind his mother's skirts. A sound behind him made Brogan stand to one side as the four Thompsons pushed past, all well aware that their reputations in the community had taken yet another dent. They turned round a corner and were lost from sight. Brogan was joined by Mick Fletcher.

'That sure was some pretty footwork,' he said, 'but do you reckon you could've taken the four of them?'

'Probably,' grinned Brogan, rather boastfully.

'How about them?' Mick nodded at three young women who had just come into town on the same buckboard Brogan had seen earlier. 'Jane, May an' Betty, the three daughters. Don't be fooled by their pretty looks, all three of 'em are just as hard as their brothers, maybe even harder, an' I hear they're all good shots an' not afraid to use a gun if they have to.'

'If it was a case of them or me I wouldn't have no problem,' said Brogan. 'I don't much like the idea of shootin' a woman though.'

'Maybe that's what they're bankin' on,' said Mick. 'I don't like it when there's too many Thompsons of either sex in town, it usually means a whole lot of trouble.'

'All we need is for the other brothers an' Ma Thompson to come,' said Brogan.

'Me an' some others have been wonderin' about that,' said Mick. 'I can only recall it happenin' once before that anyone gave them much trouble an' then they all turned up, surrounded the feller and blasted him full of holes. We was thinkin' that maybe that's what they would do with you.'

'And all of you would just stand there

and let 'em do it,' sneered Brogan. 'Now if I was sheriff, maybe I could order some of you to help me.'

'You could try,' grunted Mick. 'The last one had the same idea but when he found himself on his own he backed off. I guess we should've stood by him but none of us was prepared to die for either him or Riverdale.'

By that time the three women had been joined by their brothers and the previously large crowd suddenly disappeared as people remembered that they had far more important business to attend. However, Brogan was aware of a great many eyes staring at them from behind darkened windows. Brogan was obviously the topic of conversation between the Thompsons as all glanced at him from time to time. Eventually the three women laughingly crossed the steet, heading straight for him. Brogan touched the brim of his hat as one of them spoke.

'You stink!' announced one of them

sniffing the air and who appeared to be the eldest. 'But then all saddlebums stink. I hear you just made fools of our brothers an' not for the first time.'

'Yeh,' said another, 'only wish we could've been around to see it. They need takin' down a few pegs. They're just like all men, think they're the greatest thing there ever was.'

'I'm surprised you talk about your brothers like that,' smiled Brogan. 'Mind, your pa talks that way about 'em too. Anythin' I can do for you ladies?'

All three laughed and the eldest spoke. 'Ladies he calls us! We ain't no ladies; we're Thompsons an' proud of it. Mind, it does have its drawbacks; look at us, in our twenties an' not yet married. The trouble is there ain't no man in the territory who is prepared to take on a Thompson woman. I'd say you wasn't married Mister McNally, do you fancy takin' on one of us? I'm Jane, the eldest, so I'd say I got first claim.' She laughed. 'Pa sure would be pleased, he'd more'n forgive you for the trouble you've given him so far, an' you don't seem a bad-lookin' feller, a bit old maybe but better'n nothin' an' I reckon a good bath will improve things.'

'You just ruined any chance you might've had,' said Brogan. 'Why is it that all women just seem to want to get a man in a bath? Anyhow, it seems to me that all the trouble has been caused by your brothers.'

'Very likely,' agreed another sister. 'No, short of marryin' one of us, there ain't nothin' you can do. We only came into town to take a look at this stranger who managed to make idiots of our brothers. We probably won't see you again, you'll be dead.'

'So everyone keeps tellin' me,' grinned Brogan. 'In fact they've been sayin' it so long that I think they almost believe it. Pardon me if I don't agree; it seems to me I've been here before in another time an' another place an' as you can see, my stinkin' body is still here.'

'Maybe you've been dead for years an' don't realize it,' laughed Jane Thompson. 'That smell could just be your body rottin' away.'

At that moment Billy Morgan—Daft Billy—struggled up on to the boardwalk and grinned at Brogan holding his twisted hand out to him. Brogan deliberately took the hand although he did not really want to. It was more in a way of a gesture to show the Thompson women that forcing Billy to dance was not the way to treat him. Jane Thompson, grimaced and pulled away.

'Ugh!' she grated. 'Get him away from me. He shouldn't be allowed out, he ought to be kept in a cage.'

'He should've been destroyed at birth!' muttered another sister.

'He can't help bein' the way he is,' said Brogan. 'There sure ain't no harm in him. All this trouble with your brothers started 'cos they was shootin' at his feet to make him dance an' I stopped 'em.'

'Maybe he can't help the way he is,' said Jane, 'but he still gives a whole lot of folk the creeps; you ask anyone in town.' That was something Brogan had discovered to be true, even with someone like Madge Jones. As well as Mick Fletcher not allowing Billy into the saloon, Madge Jones had a rule banning him from her eating-house and it seemed that he was also banned from all the stores.

Silas Morgan, Billy's grandfather, came along the boardwalk and took hold of his grandson's hand and led him away with the comment that they ought to thank the Good Lord that they weren't like him.

'Well, it's been nice meetin' you, Mr McNally,' said Jane. 'Maybe you are a bit too old to be my husband but if you want to think about it, I'm prepared to listen.'

'Accordin' to you an' most folk round here I'll be dead before too long,' grinned Brogan, 'so there don't seem much point in even thinkin' about it.'

'You could be right,' she smiled. All three pushed past and made their way to the general store.

In the meantime the four brothers had led their horses down the street, apparently heading towards the river. There was nothing unusual in this, a lot of the townsfolk used the large pool below the wooden bridge to bathe in the heat of the day and some even tried their luck at fishing. The idea of voluntarily immersing one's body in water was something Brogan could never understand. The nearest he normally came to such a thing was to splash the occasional drop on to his face and claim it as a wash. He returned to the stable and threw himself down on a pile of straw. That was more his style, relaxing amongst the fleas and ticks. However, it might have appeared that he was asleep but, as ever, his senses were on the alert.

FOUR

How long he had been asleep, Brogan was not certain and it did not really matter since he had nothing else to do. It was still daylight and he guessed probably about five o'clock. What roused him was a sudden burst of gunfire, gunfire which continued sporadically over the next few minutes. From the pattern of shots and even the sound, he guessed that there was no gunfight going on, but that someone, possibly two or three of them, were either firing at targets or simply doing a bit of hell-raising. He was inclined to think the latter.

At first he was determined to stay where he was and ignore the situation. He thought that it was probably the Thompson boys letting the town know that they were still in charge and it really was no concern of his; the relationship between the people of Riverdale and the Thompsons was quite definitely their problem. No matter what happened between him and the Thompsons in the short term, when he had left or possibly had been killed, the townsfolk would still have to come to terms with the fact that his passage through the town had been little more than a brief diversion and he rather resented being treated as a diversion, especially by seemingly ungrateful townsfolk. He had been thinking about the situation and had reached the conclusion that in this case his intervention would achieve nothing. However, his desire to stay out of what was happening at that moment was changed when Silas Morgan panted his way into the stable and held himself up by leaning against a partition.

'They're at it again!' he wheezed. 'They're plaguin' Billy again.'

'Then why don't one of you stop 'em?'

suggested Brogan, chasing a few fleas around his body.

'One of us!' exclaimed Silas. 'How the hell are we supposed to do that? There ain't a man or woman in town who really knows how to handle a gun of any kind an' most, if not all, includin' me an' Walter, would probably freeze up if they pointed a gun at a human bein'. They could kill deer or rabbit an' not even think about it but put another man in their sights ... The last man, apart from you, who tried to stop the Thompsons doin' anythin' ended up in one of the best spots in the cemetery.'

'I ain't so sure about Walter,' said Brogan. 'He don't seem scared of 'em.'

'And he ain't no gunman either,' said Silas. 'None of us is. The nearest thing most of us have to a gun is maybe an old rifle or a shotgun. Even them that have ain't used 'em in years an' they might not even work. Anyhow, right now he's out at the Fisher place seein' to one of their horses. He's the nearest thing we have to a veterinarian in Riverdale. Pretty good too. Anyhow, even if he was here I don't think he'd do anythin', he's got a wife an' three kids to think about.'

'If the Thompsons are that bad, why ain't you called in a US marshal?' asked Brogan.

Silas shook his head. 'That's simple,' he said. 'This territory ain't in the Union, so a US marshal don't have the authority. We even asked the governor of the territory for help but he just didn't want to know.'

'So the only person in town it don't really matter if he gets killed or not is me. Get McNally to do it, he's only a dirty old saddlebum, nobody ain't goin' to miss him if he gets himself killed.' Brogan was becoming quite angry, something which he rarely did. 'Mister Morgan,' he continued. 'I'm sorry for a kid like Billy, believe me, I really am, but I can't be here all the time to hold his hand or get anyone else in this town out of the shit, an' I don't intend to. All I was doin' was passin' through when

I happened to see a bunch of hooligans teasin' a cripple. If I had had any sense at the time I would've ignored 'em. Instead, it seems that I've upset someone called Thompson an' they're out to kill me even though I've done nothin' more'n put one of them out of action for a while. If you folk can't get yourselves organized to deal with the Thompsons then don't expect anyone else to do it for you. I'm leavin' town in the mornin' no matter what happens. They could murder the whole town for all I care, it still wouldn't be none of my business.'

Silas looked amazed and open mouthed as Brogan let off steam. Eventually he nodded and slowly turned to leave. 'I got me an old handgun somewheres,' he said. 'Last time I used it was about twenty years ago, but I guess it might still work an' I might be able to handle it.' He stopped by the door and looked at Brogan. 'You is right, young feller,' he nodded. 'This ain't none of your business: we have to sort things out ourselves. Thanks for what you did for Billy anyhow, there ain't many folks, especially strangers, who would raise a finger to help anyone, let alone someone like Billy.' He turned again and left the stable. Brogan shrugged and sat down in the straw, idly chewing at a dry strand. The shooting began again and suddenly Brogan was on his feet, adjusting his gunbelt and then checking that both his rifle and Colt were loaded.

'McNally!' he shouted at himself. 'When the hell are you gonna learn not to poke your big nose into other folk's business? One day you're gonna regret it an' end up bein' buzzard meat.' He laughed at himself. 'I guess if you did you wouldn't know a damned thing about it.' He patted his horse. 'If I ain't back soon, you look after yourself.' She looked at him with big, brown eyes and snorted slightly and then nuzzled his side. He patted her again and walked out. The shooting was still going on, although with less frequency than before and now he could hear the sound of female voices cheering. He needed no second guesses as to who it was doing the cheering.

He did not hurry up the side street from the smithy but he was well aware that he had been seen almost as soon as he had left. He knew that the word would be quickly passed to the Thompsons and it seemed that the shooting intensified the closer he got. There were brief lulls when he knew that they would be reloading and he began to wonder just how much ammunition the brothers had. However, he was not too worried about Billy Morgan, he doubted if they would deliberately hurt him, but there was always the danger of an accident, and as far as ammunition was concerned, the more they shot, the fewer bullets they would have when he got there.

He chose not to approach them along the main street, which was what they would expect, and he rarely chose to do what was expected of him. Instead he went along a narrow alley behind one of the stores which, he guessed, would eventually bring him out almost opposite the saloon, from where the shooting appeared to be coming. He was right; after a couple of turns the alley did come out almost opposite the saloon and since they must have been expecting him along the street, nobody saw him make his way up the alley and stand behind a large water butt.

He had not taken much notice of Silas Morgan when he had said that he had an old gun somewhere and he had certainly never dreamt for one moment that the old man would actually try to use it, but, as he watched from the alley, the shooting suddenly stopped and Billy ceased jumping up and down and the women became silent. All heads turned to look down the street and the three women started to laugh and jeer.

'Leave him alone!' shouted Silas. 'What the hell has he ever done to you? Leave him alone or I'll kill the next one who shoots at him.'

'Are you sure you know which end the bullet comes out of?' called a voice.

'I know enough to be able to kill you,' called the old man. 'Now, do like I say an' leave him alone.'

'You want him, you come an' get him,' said another voice. 'Maybe you can dance better'n him. Come on, old man, show us how they used to dance in the old days.'

Brogan tensed as, very stupidly, Silas raised the gun and fired. The shot was surprisingly accurate for such an old weapon and fired by a man who claimed that he had not used a handgun for twenty years, shattering a post close to where Frank Thompson stood. It obviously surprised Frank as well. He raised his gun.

'That was a stupid move, old man,' he grated. 'I was kinda hopin' that your friend the saddlebum would be here. We heard he was on his way but it seems he's shit scared an' changed his mind probably hidin' somewhere hopin' we won't find him. You shouldn't've done that. No man shoots at a Thompson an' lives, not even stupid old men like you. Now you die an' who's goin' to look after Billy then ...?' He steadied his gun but it was Silas who responded first by firing another shot which thudded into the wall behind Frank, temporarily making him lower his gun. He snarled something and raised the gun again, clutching it with both hands to ensure accuracy.

There was a single shot, but it was not Silas Morgan who fell to the ground, it was Frank Thompson. Brogan's shot, with his rifle, had been deadly accurate and he was quite satisfied that this time his target was dead. He knew the bullet had shattered the man's skull.

Nobody seemed to know just where the shot had come from and surprisingly, Brogan thought, the three women screamed and ran for cover. The other three brothers also dived behind the nearest cover and for a few moments an unnatural silence descended. Silas Morgan too seemed to be in a daze and he simply stood in the middle of the street looking bewildered and staring first at the body of Frank Thompson and then at the ancient gun in his hand as if he was somehow convinced that it had been he who had fired the fatal shot. Billy had seated himself on the steps of the saloon and was laughing inanely and slowly clapping his hands. There was nothing Brogan could do about him but of all of them he considered that Billy was probably in the least danger.

'Move out of the way, Silas,' called Brogan. 'An' you other Thompsons, don't even think about killin' the old man. The first one who fires a shot in his direction ends up a dead man.'

'Show yourself, McNally!' called out Wilbur Thompson. 'Face us like a man.'

'Now that would be very foolish of me,' laughed Brogan. 'I know we all have to die sometime but I don't believe in volunteerin' to be executed.'

'Just like all saddlebums,' called Wilbur, 'a damned great yeller streak runnin' right up your back.'

'OK,' laughed Brogan, 'I'll agree with that. It don't bother me none to be called names. Lots of folk have done that before an' most of 'em is dead now but I'm still alive, yeller or not. Talkin' about facin' somebody like a man, how's about your steppin' out from behind that trough an' facin' me?' There was a mouthful of colourful, abusive language from Wilbur but he did not take up the suggestion. 'I guess you just found a yeller streak up your back too,' continued Brogan, laughing. 'Now, I don't really want to have to kill any more of you, so you can come out from where you're hidin' an' collect your brother. I guess your pa will be mighty sore with you, I know kids like you are allus losin' things but it is very careless of you to lose a brother.'

'Before today,' called Wilbur, 'if you

had left town, we probably wouldn't've bothered goin' after you, even though you did shoot Carl. Things is different now though, killin' Frank was the dumbest move you ever made. You just signed your death warrant.'

'So I was expected to just stand by an' let Frank shoot the old man?' said Brogan. 'Believe me, I know that's what he was goin' to do, I've seen that look in a man's eyes before.'

'Sure, he was goin' to kill him,' agreed Wilbur. 'He had to, the old fool was too dangerous. If we'd let him get away with it other folk might've had ideas about shootin' at us too. Even if you ain't dead—which you will be—you can't hang around forever, you can't protect him or anyone else in town for ever. When you're gone things'll go back to how they were except that old Silas will be livin' in the cemetery.'

Brogan was well aware that what Wilbur said was very true, nothing would really change and he even started to regret not having remained in the stable and ignoring everything. But, he had not and he had now killed one of the Thompson brothers and that alone was sufficient to ensure that they doubled their efforts to kill him.

'You can take Frank,' said Brogan. 'You put your guns away an' I'll do the same an' I'll step out into the street where you can see me, or do you want to carry on until more of you are dead?' There was a brief silence before Wilbur replied.

'You got yourself a deal,' he eventually agreed. 'The only thing I can say to you is if you want to stand any chance of livin' you put as much distance between Riverdale an' yourself as possible as soon as we leave town.'

'I was thinkin' of leavin' anyhow,' said Brogan. 'OK. We all step out into the street together.'

Three figures very slowly stood up, their arms akimbo to show that they were unarmed and Brogan too stepped from behind the water butt and out from the alley, his arms also wide of his body and unarmed. By that time Silas had come out of his daze and, on seeing the three Thompson brothers, shakily raised his gun.

'Don't be so stupid, Silas,' yelled Brogan. The old man turned, saw Brogan and lowered the gun. 'Take Billy home,' continued Brogan. 'I reckon he's had enough excitement for one day.' The three brothers had stopped and were ready to draw their guns but none of them was prepared to make the first move, having seen just how fast Brogan was on the draw. The old man shook his head, looked briefly at his gun before slipping it into the top of his trousers and then going across to Billy.

When the pair had walked away, the brothers relaxed a little and went to the body of their brother, around whose head a swarm of flies had already gathered.

By that time quite a few of the citizens

of Riverdale had appeared, seemingly from cracks in walls and holes in the ground, like so many ants, and were now standing around—at a discreet distance—gawping at Brogan and the body of Frank Thompson. Most had seen dead bodies before, but this was the first time any of them had seen a dead Thompson. Two of the sisters also appeared but the third, Jane, the eldest, was not to be seen and Brogan appeared not to notice this fact. The brothers picked up Frank's body and heaved it on to the buckboard which stood close by, although the horse had been put out on to a patch of grass behind the saloon and loosely tethered, as had the four horses belonging to the brothers. This was something most visitors to Riverdale did if they were staying some time.

Brogan stayed where he was, at the end of the alley, and idly watched as the horses were led from the patch of grass, the one horse fitted with drawing harness for the buckboard and saddles thrown across three of the others. Frank's horse was tethered to the rear of the buckboard.

It may have appeared to everyone that Brogan was watching the activities of the brothers with the attitude of a man who was ready to spring into action if one of them dared to make a wrong move, but at that moment it was not the brothers or the two younger sisters who concerned him, it was the whereabouts of the eldest sister, Jane.

It was the briefest of movements and the faintest of sounds which gave her position away and suddenly Brogan was twisting round and was down on one knee. There was a single shot followed by a shrill scream of pain. As soon as Brogan had moved, Wilbur had snatched his gun from his holster and fired at the crouching Brogan. Once again Brogan twisted round ...

Brogan's first shot had slammed into the shoulder of Jane Thompson, the force of it sending her crashing to the ground and the handgun she had, firing harmlessly into the ground as she dropped it. Wilbur's shot skimmed past Brogan's shoulder and into the side of the building behind him. Brogan's next shot also slammed into Wilbur's arm, making him drop his gun. The other brothers and sisters hardly moved. This sudden activity made all the ants who had previously crawled out of the woodwork and holes in the ground make a dash for safety.

'That wasn't very wise of your sister,' called Brogan. 'She's OK, but she has a mighty sore shoulder. You was lucky too, Wilbur. I could easily have killed you.' That statement was made more out of bravado than anything else, he had in fact simply fired blind and had been lucky to even hit Wilbur. Fortunately the others believed him.

Brogan put his gun away and went to Jane Thompson and helped her to her feet. She looked at him with hatred for a moment and then suddenly spat in his face. Brogan simply ignored the incident and pushed her out into the street where she was immediately besieged by her sisters, each trying to attend her wound. It was very noticeable that Wilbur was left to his own devices.

Eventually the horses were either saddled or harnessed to the buckboard and, with both Wilbur and his sister, Jane, letting Brogan know in no uncertain manner with some very choice language that his time on earth was definitely limited, they left town.

As soon as the Thompsons had disappeared from sight, the woodwork and holes in the ground opened up again and the citizens of Riverdale turned out to view the man who had taken on the Thompsons and won—so far. The general consensus was still that this strange saddletramp could not beat the combined might of the Thompsons. Shortly after the excitement had died down, Walter Morgan came back into town driving his wagon.

'It looks like I missed all the excitement,' he said to Brogan. 'I ain't complainin' though.'

Brogan told Walter what had happened with his father and when he had finished Walter shook his head sadly. 'He threatened to kill one of them once before,' he said. 'He even got as far as gettin' out that old gun of his but I took it off him. I wish I'd been around this time too.'

'Maybe it was my fault,' said Brogan. 'He came to me for help an' I told him that I wasn't goin' to an' that it was up to the folk of Riverdale to sort out their own problems. Mind, I still stand by that. I'm leavin' tomorrow no matter what happens so from then on you're all on your own.'

Walter sighed and nodded. 'You're right, of course. We have to stand up to the Thompsons some time, so it might as well

97

be sooner rather than later. Fortunately for us and unfortunately for him, you've got rid of one of the worst, young Frank, but to be quite honest, if it was only the boys I don't think we would have a problem. The real problem is Jimmy Thompson, he's unpredictable an' very dangerous.'

'And he'll be even more dangerous as soon as he hears about his son,' said Brogan. 'If I was you I'd arrange with other folk in town to post a lookout tonight, it wouldn't surprise me if they came in after dark. They'll be after me, of course, but if they can't find me, they could just take it out on other folk.'

'I think a lot of folk are ahead of you, Brogan,' smiled Walter, pointing at two wagons which had suddenly appeared. Both were loaded with whatever valuables could be loaded and each carried a whole family. Walter stopped the first wagon and spoke to the man holding the reins. 'What's happening?' he asked.

'We're movin' up country for a while,' replied the man. 'We is off to stay with my brother an' the Smiths—' he nodded behind at the other wagon—'they're off to that cabin he owns in the forest. He reckons he'd rather face a whole family of bears with sore heads than stay here while the Thompsons are in this mood. He's right too. There's a few others packin' up right now. If the Thompsons can be got rid of we'll be back, but not before.' He urged his team of two mules forward.

'We've had trouble with the Thompsons for years,' said Walter, sighing, as he watched the wagons disappear in the opposite direction to where the Thompsons lived, 'but I've never seen folk so damn scared. Before it's always been a case of the Thompsons gettin' their own way an' leavin' folk alone, apart from Billy. They've always teased him, but now, since you arrived an' shown the Thompsons for what they really are, they're all runnin' scared. They know that when you're either dead or gone on your way, the Thompsons will run riot an' there won't be nobody to stop 'em.'

'It would seem that all your present problems could have been solved if I had just raised my hands and let 'em shoot me,' said Brogan. 'Sorry, Walter, but you'd made your own problems long before I reached Riverdale.' At that moment both Mick Fletcher and Chas Brown rushed across the street, calling to Brogan.

'McNally!' called Chase Brown as he puffed heavily towards them. 'You can't leave town now, you can't leave us to the Thompsons, not after what you've done.'

'After what I've done!' exclaimed Brogan. 'I suppose it don't matter what they tried to do to me? As for leavin' town, you just wait an' see. I might even leave tonight but one thing's certain: I sure as hell won't be here in the mornin'.'

'There are some who say that you're

runnin' scared,' said Mick Fletcher, hastily adding, 'not that I agree with 'em of course, but you can't stop folk talkin'.'

'We need you, McNally,' said Chas. 'Without you this town is doomed. The Thompsons will slaughter us all if they can't get at you and they still might even if they can ...'

'That just about says it all!' snapped Brogan. 'It ain't me or my ability you want, all you want is for me to stay around in the hope that the Thompsons will kill me and be satisfied.' Chas Brown and Mick Fletcher looked uneasily at each other. 'Well, I got news for you, all of you, Brogan McNally don't make himself a human sacrifice for nobody. I was just sayin' to Walter that if you had any sense you'd post someone out of town where they could see the Thompsons comin' say at the bridge. They could fire a warnin' shot an' you would be ready. I might be wrong but I reckon they will be back in town after dark.'

'And you'll be gone?' said Chas. 'I hope you have a conscience, McNally. The slaughter of a lot of innocent folk will be on your hands.'

'That kind of sentiment don't work with me,' grated Brogan. 'If there was just one person in this town who genuinely cared what happened to me, I might—and only might—think about it. Hell, man, there must be about two hundred folk. Don't tell me that you can't get yourselves organized properly. There's only seven of the Thompsons now, one's dead an' one is out of action.'

'That's easier said than done,' protested Chas. 'Most folk just don't want to take the risk.'

'Half a dozen of you then,' sighed Brogan. 'Surely you can find six people?'

'Maybe,' nodded Mick. 'That's about all though an' since you won't help, I guess we've got no option.'

'That's right,' said Brogan. 'You don't have no option.'

FIVE

Brogan did give very serious thought to leaving town that night, but a combination of logic—often rare in his thinking—and a very strong element of pure pig-headedness made him delay his departure. His first act after the Thompsons had left town was to go along to Madge's Eatin'-House and order a large portion of her delicious steak pie followed by apple pie. Of all the people in town Madge appeared to be just about the only one who agreed with everything Brogan had done so far and did not seem frightened of what the Thompsons might do and who also accepted that the town as a whole would have to do something once he had gone.

'They all needed somethin' or somebody to give them a good kick in the pants,' she said. 'Me an' Walter have been telling them so for years. The trouble has been that two voices don't carry that much weight. Maybe now they'll listen a bit more, especially Chas Brown, he's just about the biggest fence sitter I've ever come across.'

'Well,' said Brogan as he finished off his apple pie and took hold of the large mug of coffee. 'From tomorrow mornin' Riverdale is definitely on its own as far as I'm concerned. There's only one thing I'm goin' to miss an' that's your wonderful cookin'.' He drank some coffee and smacked his lips. 'I make coffee sometimes but it never tastes like this, I must be doin' somethin' wrong somewheres.'

'Good quality coffee,' she said. 'You probably get passed off with inferior stuff, they think you don't know any different.'

'They is right too,' he grinned. 'Coffee is coffee as far as I'm concerned.'

'Did I hear you saying something to

Chas about posting a lookout by the bridge tonight?' Brogan nodded. 'Knowing Chas I'd say he hasn't done a damned thing about it either,' she continued. 'Do you really think they will try something?'

'I sure wouldn't be surprised,' he nodded. 'They'll be after me but if they don't find me they just might turn nasty with other folk.'

'Will they find you?' she asked.

'Not if I can help it,' he said with a grin. She did not ask how he was going to avoid them.

Feeling very pleasantly full, and since he had little else to do at that moment, Brogan drifted across the street and into the saloon where he bought a large beer and a packet of cheroots. He did not smoke that often but there were times when he really enjoyed one, besides which he always liked to have some in his saddle-bag. A lighted cheroot was just about the only effective way of removing ticks from his or his horse's body.

There were about twenty other customers in the saloon and all looked rather apprehensive as he entered and there were mutterings about being safer outside, but none actually left. There were various games of cards in progress but Brogan was not invited to join any—not that he wanted to. In fact it appeared that nobody was prepared to even talk to him for fear of being labelled by the Thompsons as being in league with him and thus incurring their wrath.

'Did you or the mayor take up on my idea about keepin' watch?' he asked Mick Fletcher. He somehow knew that the answer would be in the negative.

'Gettin' folk to volunteer for anythin' in this town is almost impossible,' said Mick, confirming that nothing had been done.

'Have you tried askin'?' said Brogan.

'Waste of time,' muttered Mick. 'You don't know folk around here like we do. I reckon the only thing we can do is wait an' see what happens.'

'And if they ride in shootin' an' burnin' everythin' in sight?' prompted Brogan.

Mick shrugged. 'I've got a gun loaded an' ready under the counter. I can't speak for anyone else.'

Brogan shook his head and sighed. 'That's the trouble with everyone in this town, you don't get together, you don't talk about it an' you sure don't act together. Look at you, all you say is that you have a gun ready if you should need it. How many other folk have guns ready just in case they need one? There's probably at least a dozen folk ready to fight the Thompsons but nobody knows the other eleven even exist. Unless you all get together—you know, call a meetin' of everyone in town an' maybe even the surroundin' farms—an' get yourselves organized you ain't never goin' to beat a kid with a cork gun let alone the Thompsons.'

'That's why we need someone like you as sheriff,' grumbled Mick. 'You could organize things like that.'

'And why can't somebody like you or Walter Morgan do it?' said Brogan. 'You ain't babes in arms who have to be wet-nursed, you're all grown men. Anyhow, from tomorrow mornin' you is definitely on your own an' as far as I see it you can either get yourselves organized or move to some other part of the country. You might as well, you sure don't have much of a future here as long as you give way to the Thompsons all the time.'

'Yeh, yeh, McNally!' said Mick. 'It's all very well for someone like you to talk so big, you just don't know the folk around here.'

Brogan turned and looked at the other customers for a few moments. 'They don't seem no different to folk I seen in other towns,' he said. 'Have you ever asked any of 'em exactly what they think?' Mick shook his head. 'I thought not,' continued Brogan. 'OK, I'll ask 'em, there's a pretty good cross section of folk in here right now.' He turned and called out, 'Listen, you folk,' he said, 'I know you all got problems with the Thompsons in one way or another an' I know there's a good many of you blame me for what's happened in the last couple of days ...'

'We might've been better off if you hadn't shown your face here,' commented one. 'At least the Thompsons were only an irritation we could put up with.'

'OK,' agreed Brogan, 'I'll go along with that, but the fact is I did ride into town an' I did stop 'em teasin' Billy Morgan an' I did shoot Carl Thompson an' I did kill Frank. Them's the facts, facts none of us can do nothin' about now. Now I aim to ride out of here in the mornin' no matter what happens, but me leavin' town ain't goin' to alter nothin'. At best things'll just go back to how they were before. Is that what you all want? I was tellin' Mick here, an' Chas Brown, that what you have to do is get yourselves organized, get together an' put up a front against the Thompsons. I've seen it all before an' you can believe me when I say that if folk like the Thompsons are presented with other folk who are determined not to allow trouble, they soon back down.'

'We need a sheriff,' said another man. 'We need someone who is prepared to stand up to the Thompsons, with the backin' of the rest of the town of course. I hear that you was offered the job but turned it down.'

'I'm a drifter,' said Brogan. 'I would've thought it was obvious to all of you that I'm a saddletramp. I ain't ashamed of that tag. It's true, I am a saddletramp, but not all of us are thieves an' robbers an' such like. I don't expect any of you to believe that this is one saddlebum who ain't never stole nothin' off nobody, never raped a woman an' never murdered a man in cold blood. Sure, like today, I've killed a few men but only those who deserved to die or those I killed in self-defence. The only reason I killed Frank Thompson today was 'cos his head was the only clear target I had to aim at. I couldn't take the chance of shootin' at his arms or hands, I could easily have missed an' that might've meant that old Silas Morgan would be dead by now.'

'I don't reckon there's a man here who'd be stupid enough to take on the job of sheriff,' said another. 'That'd be one sure-fire way of puttin' him in the front line for the Thompsons to shoot at. Anyhow, I don't reckon there's anyone with the know-how with guns to be much of a deterrent to even the kid with the cork gun you was talkin' about.'

'How about you?' Brogan suggested.

'Me!' exclaimed the man. 'Hell, I got me a wife an' three kids to worry about. I sure can't risk makin' my wife a widow.'

'Have you asked her how she feels about things like that?' persisted Brogan.

'Don't have to ask her anythin',' grumbled the man. 'She does as she's told.'

Brogan smiled and took another drink of his beer. 'How about the rest of you, or do you all have a wife an' three kids to worry about?'

A younger man of about twenty-five stood up and looked around at the others. 'McNally's right,' he said. 'All we do is sit here an' complain about things, about how somethin' ought to be done but nobody is ready to do anythin'. You all know me, I was born an' raised in Riverdale an' even I can remember when this was a good town to live in. The Thompsons were still around then but they weren't no trouble, at least not that I can remember. I was thinkin' very seriously of leavin' the town an' goin' some place where folk weren't afraid to do things, but I don't want to go. I ain't got no kids, not yet anyhow, but I am betrothed to marry Mary Tranter an' I know she feels the same way I do.'

'So why don't you take on the job of sheriff?' sneered another man. The young man looked at the sneerer for a moment and then round at the others before stepping forward to the counter.

'Hand me that badge, Mick,' he said. 'Sure, I'll take on the job; I for one ain't scared of the Thompsons'. There was a mixture of laughter and sneers of disbelief at the young man's statement, but Mick Fletcher did not offer him the badge.

'What the hell use would you be?' asked Mick. 'You ain't dry behind the ears yet. I'll bet you don't even own a handgun.'

'Sure do,' beamed the young man. 'It was my pa's. It ain't that modern but it's still a good gun. Anyhow, I can use a rifle better'n most men in this town. I don't know how old I have to be before some of you think I'm dry behind the ears, but I reckon if I'm old enough to take on a wife then I'm old enough to be a sheriff.'

'What about Doug Tranter, what does he think?' asked someone else. 'He's only got a daughter an' I know he was hopin' for a son-in-law to take on the runnin' of the farm when he dies or retires. If you take on the sheriff's job he's goin' to have to find someone to help out at the farm.

You owe Doug a lot, Barry; when your ma an' pa died he took you on when nobody else would ...'

'Includin' you!' interrupted Barry.

'Yeh, includin' me,' continued the man, unabashed. 'I ain't ashamed to admit it, but then I've got two sons to help me out. The point is, he's been like a father to you these past three years, you can't just walk out on him.'

'He don't really need me round the farm,' said Barry. 'OK? You're right, I do owe him, but normally there's only enough work for one man. Me an' Mary was thinkin' about leavin' Riverdale an' Doug Tranter knows it. He don't particularly like the idea but he hasn't tried to stop us, so I don't see as this would be any different.'

'Except it might make his daughter a widder woman at a very early age,' said the man.

'That's a chance I'll just have to take,' said Barry. 'I could die fallin' off a horse or somethin' stupid just like Al Simpson did last year. He'd just got married to Gwen Foster an' was ridin' into town when his horse shied at a rattler an' he was thrown off an' it was him that got bit by it an' left his Gwen a widder at twenty-two. Hell, a man could get bit by a snake every time he plants a few crops but that don't stop him plantin' those crops.'

'Yeh, well ... maybe other folk in town don't want you to be their sheriff?' objected the man. 'I know I don't.'

'So either suggest someone you do want or shut up,' said Barry. 'You're just like everyone else, all you can do is talk about things an' run like hell once any trouble starts.'

Brogan had been listening to the conversation quite fascinated. Here at last was one man, no matter how young and inexperienced, who seemed prepared to do something other than talk and complain. He looked around at the others and noted that at least half of them appeared to be in agreement with young Barry, but they generally seemed to be the younger element, those under the age of about thirty-five.

'Seems to me like you've just been made an offer you can't refuse,' Brogan said to them all. 'OK, so he ain't had that much experience, but then how many of you have? I tried bein' a sheriff once an' I didn't have no experience, but he's young an' can learn fast.' He looked at Barry and smiled. 'Have you ever raised a gun against a man?' he asked. Barry shook his head. 'It don't matter none,' continued Brogan. 'I've seen plenty of sheriffs who ain't never had to either. Some of 'em have been damned good sheriffs too. It ain't just a matter of lockin' folk up or shootin' 'em, there's all sorts of disputes an' other problems which a sheriff has to deal with. You need someone who is willin': it's no use pressin' a man into the job, he's liable to walk out the first time there's any real trouble.'

'Just like our last sheriff,' nodded Mick Fletcher.

At that moment Chas Brown, the mayor, and Walter Morgan came into the saloon and appeared startled by the apparent debate going on. Mick Fletcher explained what had happened and the offer Barry Day had made. Walter nodded to Chas and Mick to follow him into the back room. A buzz of excitement followed their exit and a barrage of questions was aimed at Barry Day which he dealt with quite well, or so Brogan thought.

In the back room, Mick explained in greater detail what had happened. 'I reckon we've got a quorum of the town council,' said Mick. 'We can always get hold of another two if you want.'

'It was left to you or me at the last council meetin',' said Chas. 'What's your view, can we trust young Barry to do the job?'

'I would've preferred someone older,' admitted Mick, 'but the only trouble is just where are we goin' to get anybody else?'

'Me too,' said Walter. 'But he's a good lad. Hell we can hardly call him a lad now can we? He is twenty-five an' I seem to remember bein' that age myself once. If you two were anythin' like me then you knew all there was to know at that age. I'm for givin' him the opportunity if that's what he wants.'

'Me too,' agreed Chas Brown. 'If for no other reason than to show the Thompsons that we ain't scared of them.'

'There was some concern that Doug Tranter might object,' said Mick. 'He can be awkward when he wants to be. It could be that he might be dead set against his daughter marryin' a sheriff an' try to stop him.'

'Mary Tranter is twenty-one next month,' said Walter. 'She's of an age an' mind to do her own thing, but I think I see what you're gettin' at. It is just possible that she might not like the idea. It doesn't really matter what Doug thinks about it, Barry is his own man. I suggest that we ask Barry to see what Mary has to say about it. Most likely she'll want nothin' to do with it, in which case Barry won't either.'

'OK,' agreed Mick, 'I'll go along with that. There's just one thing though, McNally has said that he's leavin' town in the mornin'. If nothin' else I think we ought to ask him to stay on a while an' give Barry some tips an' maybe teach him a thing or two about handlin' a gun.'

'A good idea,' agreed Chas. 'Walter, you seem to get along better with him than we do, you suggest it to him. Tell him we'll even pay him a dollar a day.'

'I don't think the money will have much of a bearin' on it,' smiled Walter, 'but I'll ask him. I don't know that it will make much difference though, he strikes me as the kind of feller who once he's made his mind up don't change it.'

'What about young Barry?' said Chas. 'We did offer McNally seven dollars a week all found, we can't offer Barry that much.'

'Five dollars a week all found, or seven dollars a week, a house for him an' Mary an' they buy their own food,' suggested Walter. 'That don't sound too bad to me.'

'Five dollars a week and a house,' suggested Chase.

'Five dollars ain't enough to keep a wife an' probably a family on,' said Walter.

'He might not get that much money on the farm but at least neither of them have any problems about food an' lodgin'. I say seven dollars an' a house.'

'OK?' agreed Chas Brown. 'That is of course if Mary agrees to it. Personally I have my doubts. OK, let's go and talk to Barry. He could go and see Mary now; she's with my wife and some other women in the drapery story, like they always are on a Wednesday.' He smiled. 'They say all they do is natter and drink lemonade, but all I can say is that the lemonade sure makes my wife very talkative an' randy.'

'Mine too!' laughed Walter.

They came out of their meeting and the babble in the room subsided into an expectant silence as if awaiting the result of some great deliberations, which in its way it was. Chas Brown, as the mayor, took centre stage and cleared his throat.

'Friends,' he said to them all. 'On behalf of the Riverdale Town Council, Mick Fletcher, Walter Morgan and myself, in my capacity as mayor ...'

'Get on with it!' someone called. 'You like the sound of your own voice too much.'

'Ahem!' coughed Chas, nervously. 'We are prepared to take up the offer made by Barry Day for him to become our sheriff. In the normal course of events our sheriffs are elected by the town as a whole but ...'

'But if there's only one candidate there ain't no point,' said the heckler. 'Get on with it!'

'We are prepared to accept his offer,' said Chas. 'I take it there are no objections?'

There were none, not even from the man who had claimed that Barry was too young. 'Then, Barry, subject to one proviso ...'

'What the hell's a proviso?' called the heckler.

'Subject to one condition,' said Chas. 'That condition is, Barry, that you talk to your future wife and then, if she is in agreement, you can take up the job. We will discuss salary and conditions if you and she agree.'

'That sounds fair enough,' said Barry with a broad grin. 'I don't think she will object though, we've often talked about somethin' like this. When do you want to know by?'

'This evening is as good a time as any,' said Mick. 'We know she's with all the other women over at the drapery store. If you can tear her away from her lemonade long enough to get a sensible answer, you can come back an' tell us.'

'I'm on my way!' laughed Barry. He ran out of the door to cat-calls about the potency of the lemonade consumed in the drapery store.

'Mr McNally,' said Chas. 'I think Walter would like to have a few quiet words with you.' Brogan glanced at Walter who nodded and he followed him into the back room.

'I don't know how you did it,' said Walter as he closed the door, 'but you've just done in a few minutes somethin' we've been tryin' to do ever since our last sheriff ran off. Mind, I think Barry Day would definitely have been too young then, but I reckon he's old enough now.'

'At least he's willin' an' he seems keen enough,' said Brogan.

'I only hope it works,' nodded Walter. 'The thing is though, he is still young and inexperienced and we think he needs some help, both with doin' the job and learnin' how to use a handgun. As far as I know he's got about as much experience as the rest of us on that score an' that's almost nil. We were wonderin' if you would stay on a day or two just to give the lad a start.'

'From you, Walter,' said Brogan with a wry smile, 'I'll accept that in the spirit it was said. If either Chas Brown or even Mick had made that suggestion I would have suspected that the main reason was to keep me hangin' around and maybe hope to make a sacrifice of me to the Thompsons. Who knows, maybe that's what you think too.'

'I wouldn't've asked if I thought that,' assured Walter. 'I think Chas and Mick were bein' perfectly genuine when it was suggested. How about it?'

'Has anyone thought to ask young Barry if he wants a nursemaid?'

'I'd hardly call it bein' a nursemaid,' smiled Walter, 'but I know what you mean and it is just possible that Mary Tranter might say no, in which case I can't see Barry goin' against her. If that happens then forget we ever had this talk. By the way, we are prepared to pay you a dollar a day for your services.'

'A dollar a day an' meals at Madge's', grinned Brogan.

'It's a deal,' laughed Walter, much to Brogan's surprise.

'Mind,' warned Brogan. 'I ain't agreed to do it, yet. Don't be surprised if you wake up in the mornin' and find me gone.'

'I wouldn't blame you if you did go,' said Walter. 'All I ask is that you think about it.'

'I'll do that,' agreed Brogan. 'I ain't makin' no promises though.'

'Understood,' nodded Walter. 'Now, come on into the bar an' I'll buy you a drink.'

About half an hour later Barry Day sought out the three members of the town council with the news that Mary Tranter had agreed and had even suggested that the date of their wedding be brought forward providing they were given suitable accommodation. The salary of seven dollars a week and a furnished house was readily accepted by the young man.

'We've asked Mr McNally to stay on to give you some help,' said Chase. 'I hope you don't think it's because we don't think you're up to it ...'

'But you don't,' smiled Barry. 'Sure, I don't mind, I ain't too proud to admit that I'm goin' to need all the help I can get. Has he agreed?'

'Not exactly,' said Chas Brown. 'He's drinkin' with Walter Morgan right now. Why don't we go an' join them and you can ask him yourself and Mick can give you your badge as well.'

The news that Mary Tranter had agreed to her future husband taking on the job of Sheriff of Riverdale had already reached the ears of the rest of the town and suddenly the saloon was full, some of whom offered Barry their commiserations but most of them appeared to wish him well in his new job. There were those, of course, who said that they had considered taking the job on themselves but felt that they were either too old or could not really commit themselves to the job. All three town councillors said to Brogan that now they had a volunteer, it was surprising just how many other volunteers there were about, if only they had been asked.

'Mr Brown tells me that you are goin' to stay on a few days to give me a few tips,' Barry said to Brogan when the initial excitement had died down. 'I sure appreciate it, Mr McNally, I was sayin' I need all the help I can get.'

'You can call me Brogan,' said Brogan. 'I don't go much on the McNally bit, but sometimes it seems right for some folk to call me that.'

'Like Mr Brown,' smiled Barry. 'Sure, I know just what you mean.'

'Anyhow,' said Brogan. 'I ain't exactly promised to stay on, I just said I'd think about it. I'm surprised your woman agreed.'

'I knew she would,' said Barry. 'The thing that surprised me was her mother sayin' it was a good idea as well an' I see Doug Tranter, my future pa-in-law, has just walked in. I hope he goes along with it.' It transpired that Doug Tranter did think that it was a good idea.

A few minutes later Barry Day was all smiles as his badge of office was pinned on to his shirt amid loud cheers and a firm handshake from Doug Tranter. Brogan chose that moment to leave and think about his next move.

SIX

After leaving the celebrations going on in the saloon, Brogan made his way down to the river, partly out of curiosity as to whether or not the Thompsons would show up that night—in which case he was quite certain they would do so before midnight—but mainly to get away from the crowd—he always preferred being alone—and to give himself the opportunity to consider the offer which had been made. At first he was reluctant to go back on his original assertion that the coming dawn would see him riding out of Riverdale, but once again, his own pride and pure mulishness came to the fore and eventually he opted to stay. Although leaving would have been the most sensible and certainly the easiest course of action, his pride rebelled at the thought of being labelled a coward, not so much being seen as such by others, but more importanly, seeing himself as having failed and being forced to run out.

He sat on the river bank for quite a long time, exactly how long he did not know and it certainly did not matter. There was a small, crescent moon, with barely enough light to see anything, and the water looked more like a black ribbon than anything else. As ever, his senses were on the alert, alert for those sounds which did not belong and which years of conditioning had taught him to filter from the natural noises whether made by animals, birds or created by the wind.

Behind him he could hear the noisy celebrations in the saloon, even though it was at least 400 yards away, but he noted that very slowly the noise was becoming less and less until eventually, and after three wagons had crossed the bridge taking farmers and their giggling, lemonade-sodden wives back home, it ceased altogether. He rightly assumed that everyone had had their fill of drink and had turned in for the night. Having decided that it was now very unlikely that the Thompsons would come into town, he too slowly made his way back.

A solitary figure was walking slowly along the boardwalk towards Brogan and did not appear to see him until they were almost on top of each other. Brogan smiled, knowing that it was the new, young sheriff exercising his right to patrol the town at night.

'The first thing you have to learn is to use your eyes an' ears,' said Brogan as the pair met. 'I could've been anybody up to no good.'

'Eyes aren't much use in the dark,' said Barry.

'You'd be surprised,' said Brogan. 'It's amazin' what you can see in the dark. Your ears are the most important though. You need to learn to listen to what's around you. I know it's not goin' to be easy but you are country born an' bred so you ought to know certain sounds.'

'Yeh,' agreed Barry, 'I reckon I know what you mean. I guess I was indulgin' in a bit of dreamin'.'

'No harm in that,' said Brogan. 'I do it all the time. I don't think anythin' will happen tonight, I suggest you go home to your bed, tomorrow things might be very different an' you'll get your first real taste of sheriffin'.'

'I got the key to the office,' said Barry, proudly. He took it out of his pocket and showed it to Brogan as if it were some form of hard-won trophy. 'I'll be sleepin' in there tonight.'

'I feel safer already,' said Brogan, patting him on the back. 'I'll see you in the mornin'.'

'Does that mean you're stayin'?'

'Guess so,' said Brogan. They bade each other a good night and went their respective ways.

There seemed to be a new sense of purpose about Riverdale the following morning, people appeared to be a little more friendly than they had been and when Barry Day, the new sheriff, appeared, it seemed that many folk went out of their way to greet him, even though everyone had known him for years. There were a few who thought that perhaps he was a little young for the job, but the general consensus was that he was a good lad and honest, which appeared to be the most important consideration. For a brief few hours it seemed that the Thompsons had been forgotten.

Brogan had a breakfast of ham and eggs in Madge's and commented that he could quite easily become very used to this life, but he was brought back to reality when Madge suggested that it might not be a bad idea if he did stay and that she could arrange for him to have a bath and get himself cleaned up. After telling her in no uncertain terms that soap and hot water were unnatural and asking her why it was most women seemed to have a fetish about getting men into water, he resolved to leave at the earliest opportunity. Since he had promised Barry Day that he would help him out for a while, Brogan decided that he would give it a week at the absolute outside.

The fact that the Thompsons had not invaded town the previous night had somewhat surprised him. He did think that they would be so riled up about the death of Frank that nothing would stop them but as they had not, he thought that it was more than likely that Jimmy, the father, had stopped them doing so. However, he had no doubts that this day would not pass without the Thompsons visiting town, and he was right.

It was a little after ten o'clock in the morning when a small boy breathlessly raced from the direction of the river where, apparently, the local school teacher had taken her class. The boy ran to the hardware store where he told Chas Brown, the mayor, that the Thompsons were on their way. From the bridge across the river there was a good view of the trail to the Thompson farm and anyone could be seen at least half a mile away. Chas Brown had immediately dashed from his store into the sheriff's office and both had seen Brogan as they came out into the street.

'They're comin'!' gasped Chas when they confronted Brogan. 'What're you goin' to do?'

'What am I goin' to do?' said Brogan. 'Nothin'; why the hell should I? You got yourselves a brand new sheriff to deal with things like that.'

'It's you they want,' objected Chas. 'It was you who killed Frank.'

By that time word had spread rapidly that the Thompsons were on their way and apparently in force and the previous sense of well-being very quickly evaporated and the streets miraculously cleared. The school class by the river had been hurried back to the schoolroom and some anxious mothers were still in the process of taking their children home.

'I'll deal with it,' said the new sheriff. 'They have to know that they can't just ride into town and do what they like whenever they want to. Brogan, I'd appreciate it if you were out of sight; they might get the message a bit quicker if you aren't around.' Brogan smiled and nodded, he did not mind at all, but at the same time he positioned himself where he could see what was going on and where he could do something if really necessary—in Madge's small dining-room.

The eventual arrival of the Thompsons, two of the daughters and Mrs Thompson riding a wagon with what appeared to be a coffin on the back, proved to be something of a surprise to everyone in that they were all, without exception, dressed in their Sunday clothes. There were two obvious absentees, Carl and Jane, the eldest son and daughter. Brogan assumed that Frank Thompson was making the journey in the rough, wooden coffin. Jimmy Thompson called his family to a halt when they were confronted by Barry Day who made certain that they saw his badge of office.

'Well now,' said Jimmy Thompson, 'what have we here? It looks like they've found someone to take on the job of sheriff. Are you sure you know just what you're doin', young Barry?'

'Yes, sir,' responded the new sheriff. 'I'm sheriff round here now and I'm not afraid to carry out the duties expected of me.'

'Then I suggest the first thing you do is arrest that saddletramp, McNally,' said Jimmy. 'He murdered my son.'

'Mr McNally was defendin' Silas Morgan,' said Barry. 'I saw it with my own eyes. If he hadn't done it I'd be arrestin' Frank for murder now.'

'Son,' said Jimmy, leaning forward slightly and staring at Barry. 'I ain't got no objection to havin' you as a sheriff, in fact I've often said we need one, but don't get yourself involved in things you ain't got no control over. Do your sheriffin', keep law an' order by lockin' up drunks an' makin' sure folk pay for any damage they cause, but don't even think about comin' between me, my family, an' that no-good saddletramp. Once he's disposed of I'll go along with almost anythin' you say as sheriff, just so long as you remember which of us is the real power round here.'

'Your days of power are over, Mr Thompson,' said Barry. 'If you or any of your family step out of line I'll take great pleasure in lockin' you up.'

'There ain't no jail strong enough to hold a Thompson!' growled Jimmy. 'Now, Sheriff, stand aside while we take the body of my son to be buried. That's all we've come into town for today, to bury Frank an' to pay our last respects to a good son.' He looked about and eventually called out, 'I know you're watchin' me, McNally, I can feel them eyes of yours. Just remember this, from now on there ain't no place you can run, no place you can hide. From now on there's goin' to be a Thompson followin' you everywhere you go until the day you die which, believe me, will be very soon. Make the most of it while you can, McNally.'

Brogan could not resist stepping out into the street and as he did so three of the brothers made brief movements towards their guns, but Brogan was ahead of them.

'You could make it a family funeral if you want,' said Brogan. 'I'd be only too happy to oblige.'

'I bet you would!' growled Jimmy, motioning his sons to put away their guns. 'You're good, fast, an' mean enough. In another life I could have admired a man like you, but I don't admire no man who murders my son. For now, McNally, you can live a while longer, right now I'm not lookin' for your blood. We are here to bury my son so kindly allow us our grief, but remember, from now on you had better be on the lookout for a Thompson wherever you go. My boys are probably surprised that you're still around but I'm not; you must be either very stupid, brave or very sure of yourself, I haven't decided which.'

'I ain't decided that either,' said Brogan. 'I've often asked myself that same question when folk like you have just told me my days are numbered. As you can see, I'm still here. OK, go ahead and have your funeral, at least it shows you've still got some decency in you.' Jimmy Thompson grunted something and waved his small cortege forward, all of whom scowled threateningly at Brogan as they passed. Word of the funeral spread rapidly throughout the town and within minutes almost the entire population had turned out to do nothing more than stand and stare. There were two regular grave-diggers whom Jimmy Thompson paid and he even managed to secure the services of the nearest person Riverdale had to a priest or ordained preacher at that moment, Samuel Bennet, a lay-preacher and Corn and Seed Merchant, who led the town in most of their services, although marriages were always conducted by the mayor.

Although he had little time for the Thompsons, Brogan felt slightly sad and even disgusted that people should be so insensitive as to intrude upon the grief of others as if it were some sort of sideshow. Barry Day, the new sheriff, apparently felt the same as he too kept his distance.

The saloon had a very busy morning. The sight of a Thompson being buried seemed to create a thirst in everyone, especially since they all believed that the Thompsons had left town again directly after the funeral. However, the babble of voices in the saloon suddenly stopped as if a tap had been turned off and a wide gap opened up between the door. Brogan and Barry Day were both at the counter. Neither of them needed any telling as to who was about to enter the saloon. The only surprise was that it was Jimmy Thompson on his own.

He looked about with a half smile, half sneer on his face as the crowd pushed back a little further and very slowly walked towards the two men at the counter. He leant alongside them, hardly giving them a glance and ordered a beer. Onlookers began to whisper, wondering just what was going to happen but the longer Jimmy leant on the counter without even glancing at Brogan or the sheriff, those whispers almost reached a crescendo.

Brogan was well aware of what was going on. He knew that Jimmy Thompson was doing exactly what he had done so often himself, stating to the world and his adversary in particular that he was not a man to be taken lightly and even issuing an unspoken challenge to his opponent.

Brogan was nearer to Jimmy Thompson and for a very brief moment there was a flash of silent communication between them, an understanding that each knew exactly what was eventually bound to happen between them. Jimmy drained his glass, smiled slightly but not actually at Brogan, turned and walked out. Immediately the babble of voices broke out again, all speculating as to what would happen next.

'What was all that about?' asked Barry. 'It was almost like two animals circlin' each other, weighin' each other up.'

'An' that's exactly what it was,' nodded Brogan. 'He knows there's only two ways this can end, either by him killin' me or me killin' him. This ain't a fight between the Thompsons an' me no more, it's a fight between just one particular Thompson an' me; Jimmy Thompson.'

'Are you worried?' asked Barry.

'What about?'

'Dyin',' said Barry. 'Bein' shot by a man like Thompson.'

'Worried about dyin'?' said Brogan. 'Naw, that never has bothered me, but he's the first man I ever met who I know is more dangerous than any other man I've ever met. There are probably men somewhere who are faster on the draw than either of us but I'll bet there ain't many who are more calculatin'. That's another thing you've got to learn, young feller, it ain't always the one who is fastest with a gun who is the more dangerous; knowin' how a man will react can save your life as easily as bein' fast. Mind, although I say it myself, someone like me or probably Jimmy Thompson who're pretty damned fast and calculatin' take some beatin'.'

'I'll go along with that,' agreed Barry. 'That's another thing I want you to teach me: how to use a gun; how to be fast on the draw and accurate.'

'Practice!' smiled Brogan. 'There's no substitute for practice. Sure, I can probably give you a few pointers, show you what you're doin' wrong an' an easy way to do things, but after that it's down to you.'

'When can we start?' asked Barry. 'I know you don't intend hangin' about much longer.'

'There's no time like the present,' replied Brogan. 'That is if the town can spare you for a couple of hours.'

'It's my own time,' smiled Barry. 'As sheriff I get to choose when I work an' when I don't. I reckon nothin' more will happen today an' I don't suppose there's anythin' else goin' on that needs my attention. What do we do first?'

'Find somewhere we won't be disturbed,' said Brogan.

'Up from the bridge is usually pretty quiet,' nodded the sheriff. 'Most folk head downstream if they're fishin' or swimmin'. It's deeper down there an' the fish are bigger.'

'Don't like fish,' said Brogan. 'I'll eat it if I have to but I don't like it much.'

'Me neither,' said Barry, 'but I used to enjoy takin' out a fishin' pole and catchin' them.'

Brogan pulled a face. 'I never did see the point of catchin' anythin' if you didn't want to eat it. Still, each to his own I suppose.'

They drained their glasses and made their way down to the river where for the next two hours Brogan instructed the new sheriff in the art of drawing and using a handgun. Barry Day was a good pupil and learnt quickly but it was obvious to Brogan that he would never completely master the art until he found himself a gun better than the rather ancient Alsop smooth bore revolver which he had inherited from his father. Apart from being rather awkward to handle, the smooth bore did not make it terribly accurate even over short distances. Barry agreed, after trying Brogan's gun and appreciating the difference, that he would have to invest in a modern Colt. For the remainder of the lesson Brogan allowed him to use his gun.

Accuracy did not appear to be a problem to the young sheriff; he seemed to have a natural eye but, like most people, his accuracy was confined to a stationary target and it was obvious that a lot more practice was required to hit a moving target. Teaching him to use his skills against a fellow human was another matter. Brogan had discovered that the vast majority of people froze when faced with the prospect of shooting at a man; it was something a man either could or could not do. Since the great majority of people were farmers or ranchers or in some way in regular employment, they normally had little need to use a gun in anger. They had lawmen to do that kind of thing for them and, as a result, as in Riverdale, guns were hardly ever worn and used even less. Someone had once told Brogan that it was only ne'er-do-wells like him who needed such skills and he had tended to agree with them.

True to his word, when they returned to the town, the first thing Barry did was to go to Chas Brown's Hardware Store, which was about the nearest thing there was to a gunsmith's in Riverdale, and ask to see the latest Colt. As it happened, Chas Brown did have one in stock, one which he had been persuaded to buy from a travelling salesman and which he was beginning to believe would never be sold.

'You can pay me weekly,' invited Chas,

knowing that the chances of the new sheriff having the ready cash for such an expensive gun were rather remote.

'I can't afford more'n one dollar a week,' said Barry. 'A sheriff's pay don't go to any more'n that.'

Rather than lose a sale, Chas Brown agreed, knowing that should anything happen to the young sheriff, he could claim the gun as being as yet unpaid for and therefore belonging to him. When it was suggested that he take the old Alsop in part exchange, he made tutting noises and pointed out that the call for handguns of any kind was almost non-existent. He did, however, offer to put the gun on display in his shop and if it should be sold, the proceeds would be set against any outstanding amount owed on the Colt—subject to a small commission. If nothing else, Charles Brown was a businessman who rarely missed an opportunity to earn a dollar.

Barry Day left the store with his new gun at his side and he seemed to be making certain that everyone noticed and it was plain that he was itching to test his new toy. Bullets presented no problem; ammunition was provided by the town and Barry had secured several boxes while in the store.

A short time after the two men left the hardware store, two of the Thompson brothers rode into town, causing consternation amongst the townsfolk, but although they scowled at both Brogan and the new sheriff, they made it plain that they were unarmed and had only been sent back to pick up some supplies. In a way, Barry felt cheated, he would have liked to have tested his new-found skills in a live situation, even though he had only had two hours of tuition.

'Don't be in too much of a hurry to die,' advised Brogan. 'You'll get your chance eventually an' if you don't, you can thank the Good Lord. Remember this: no matter how good you are, one day you'll come against someone who is even better.'

'Like you and Jimmy Thompson?' smiled Barry.

They were sitting in the reopened office, Barry searching through an old cabinet containing some maps, some official-looking forms and books which he decided he had better look at later, and a whole pile of old Wanted posters.

'No, not like me an' Jimmy Thompson,' said Brogan, also idly thumbing through some of the posters. 'I mean someone who can definitely outdraw an' outshoot you. I'm goin' to meet that feller one day, there ain't nothin' more certain. I ain't gettin' no younger and I know I must be gettin' that much slower. You keep practisin' an' you might keep one step ahead of the rest—at least for a few years.' He suddenly stopped talking and picked up a poster. 'Now lookee here!' he said. 'It seems like our Jimmy Thompson is a wanted man.' He handed the poster to Barry who whistled softly.

'Five hundred dollars!' he exclaimed. 'I could use that kind of money.'

'Can sheriffs claim the reward?' asked Brogan.

'Don't see why not,' smiled Barry. 'Five hundred dollars. Wanted for grievous assault and robbery. It don't say what he robbed though. Maybe there's somethin' about it here somewhere.' Both men began a more detailed search.

Eventually they did find a document which gave the details. It appeared that four years previously, Jimmy Thompson had been visiting the town of Cherokee Springs, in the neighbouring state, when he had become involved in a brawl during which he savagely beat a man and then robbed him of his life savings of $2,000.

'That seems straightforward,' said Barry. 'I wonder why the last sheriff didn't arrest him, maybe he was too scared of him.'

'Maybe so,' agreed Brogan. 'Well, what are you goin' to do about it? You're the law round here now.'

'Arrest him,' declared the sheriff. 'It sure ain't no use me bein' sheriff if I don't act like one.'

'Son,' said Brogan, 'I reckon before you do that you need a lot more practice with your new gun. I can't see a man like Thompson just givin' up meekly an' I can't see his sons just standin' by.'

'I have to do somethin',' said Barry. 'If I give way on this I might as well pack this job in now.'

'Let me make a suggestion,' said Brogan. 'You don't have to rush out now arrestin' nobody. Give it a week or two, maybe even longer. You have the perfect excuse of havin' to settle in an' sort out a whole pile of papers. After that, if you think you're ready, go ahead and move.'

'I'll think about it,' agreed Barry. 'I don't much like the idea of not doin' anythin', but you could be right. OK, since we're lookin', let's see if there's anyone else I know in this lot.'

It took them the best part of another hour but they did not find anything on anyone Barry knew. The only other things they found of any real interest were three bundles of legal-looking documents which Brogan discovered hidden in a false floor of a cabinet and which had apparently come from the bank, the bank now boarded up. It was obvious that an attempt had been made to hide them and it was pure chance that Brogan had pulled at a raised corner of the false floor.

They flicked through the files, which appeared to be mainly title deeds to property, but neither of them having any experience in such matters meant that they did not appreciate the significance of them. Barry decided that the only person he could ask, in the absence of a lawyer or banker in town, was the mayor, Chas Brown. The files were placed to one side but out of sight.

SEVEN

There was a verbal message waiting for Brogan when he went to Madge's for his breakfast, a rather garbled message which had apparently been relayed to Madge as Barry Day had ridden past her place just as dawn broke that morning.

'He said something about you knowing what he meant,' said Madge. 'He said something about taking the poster with him.'

'The bloody fool!' muttered Brogan. 'Sure I know what he means. How far is it to the Thompson place?'

'Best part of an hour,' she replied. As with most settlers, she judged distance in terms of time rather than miles and in a way Brogan had to admit that it made more sense in that an hour on flat, good ground, was vastly different to an hour negotiating a rocky canyon or mountain and, in a lot of cases, distances were so vast that they tended to lose all meaning. 'Is that where he's gone?' she asked.

'That's where he's gone!' sighed Brogan. 'I thought he had more sense, but he just couldn't wait. I only hope he knows what he's doin'.'

'And just what is he doing?' asked Madge. Brogan shook his head and smiled. 'OK, so it's none of my business,' she continued, 'but that future wife of his just rode into town an' if anyone has a right to know, she has. Oh, I almost forgot, he threw these keys at me and told me to give them to you. I presume they're the keys to the office.' Brogan nodded and took them.

Whilst he was eating, he thought over what he ought to do next both in terms of his own plans and the commitment he had promised to Barry Day and finally arrived at the conclusion that whatever any sheriff chose to do was nothing at all to do with him, even if he was supposed to be helping that sheriff. He finished his breakfast and went over to the office.

'Good morning,' greeted a young, good-looking woman sitting on a bench outside the office. 'Mr McNally, isn't it?'

'An' I guess you must be Miss Tranter,' smiled Brogan, touching the brim of his hat. 'I'm afraid your husband-to-be had to go out on some business early.'

'I thought he might have done,' she said. 'Do you know where to?'

'I'm only guessin',' nodded Brogan, finding the correct key to the office and opening the door, 'but I think he's out at the Thompson farm.' He held the door open and invited her into the office. 'Sorry about the mess,' he said, moving some papers off a chair and flicking his fingers over the seat in a futile attempt to clear some dust. 'We started to tidy the place up last night but we got sidetracked by some papers an' things.'

'What on earth has he gone out to the Thompsons' for?' she asked, refusing the offer of the chair and looking about with some disgust. 'You'd think someone would have made an effort to clean this place up before he moved in.'

'I ain't got the faintest idea what business he has out there,' lied Brogan. 'As for this place, I guess things happened so fast there just wasn't time. He's been sheriff less than two days so far, it took everybody by surprise. Most never expected you to agree to it.'

'It's what he wanted,' she said, running her finger across a shelf and looking in disgust at the grime sticking to the end of it. 'We were going to leave town altogether, but neither of us really wanted that; for all its faults, Riverdale is a nice place to live. I'm proud of him, proud that he alone has had the guts to take on a job everyone thought was impossible. Have you no idea why he went out to the Thompsons'?'

'None at all,' said Brogan, repeating the

lie. 'I shouldn't worry about him though; Jimmy Thompson seemed to accept the fact that he was sheriff, so I don't think he will do anything.'

'Is there any reason why he should?' she snapped, looking at him sharply. Brogan sensed that this was one very intelligent and discerning woman who saw through the lie. 'I believe you know exactly why he went out to see the Thompsons,' she said. 'Please, Mr McNally, do not treat me as a simpleton just because I am a woman. He must have discovered something about the Thompsons, something serious enough to make him go out there this morning.'

Brogan nodded, realizing that in this case, telling the truth was probably the best course of action. 'We found a Wanted poster last night ...' He started to search through the other posters on the desk. 'I don't know if there's another one here, it doesn't look like it ... Ah, what's this? Yes, there must have been two.' He handed the poster to Mary Tranter who quickly read it. 'That's why he's out there,' continued Brogan when she handed the poster back to him. 'I told him to hang back for a while, but it seems he had other ideas.'

'And he is quite right too!' she asserted. 'If he is to make a success of being the sheriff he has to show his authority. I'm proud of him. I appreciate your attempt to spare my feelings, Mr McNally, but I thank you for telling me the truth. I would have found out anyway. Now, I had intended to help him get things straightened out, but since he isn't here I suppose I shall have to do it on my own, that is unless you are willing to help, after all, I don't suppose you have anything more important to do.'

Brogan was in a corner and had to admit defeat by shaking his head in confirmation that he did not have anything better to do. She sniffed the air and looked about and finally settled her gaze on Brogan.

'I wondered where that strange smell was coming from. I suppose all men like you must smell, I understand washing and bathing are something foreign to you. It would be to most men if they were allowed to get away with it. I know I don't allow Barry to go more than two days without a bath.' She looked at Brogan and suddenly smiled. 'Don't mind me, Mr McNally, I am well known as a very plain speaker. I might not agree with your hygiene but I do appreciate what has happened to Riverdale since you turned up and I gather you are teaching Barry how to use a gun properly ...'

Brogan did wonder if she knew about the purchase of the new Colt. 'I know he needed a better gun,' she continued, confirming that she did know. 'But under the circumstances I think the council should have paid for it. I shall get my father to raise the matter; after all, it is mainly for the good of the town that he needs a decent gun.'

'I wouldn't know about things like that,' said Brogan. 'I'll ride out to the

Thompsons' and see if I can be of any help,' he suggested, feeling quite intimidated by this assertive woman who was young enough to be his granddaughter.

'You'll do no such thing!' she said very firmly. 'On his own, even if he does not succeed in arresting Jimmy Thompson for some reason, the worst thing that is likely to happen is that he will be laughed off the farm. If you were to arrive I am quite certain that it would rapidly degenerate into a gunfight, and people have been known to be killed in gunfights, as happened to Frank Thompson. You can stay here and help me get things straight.' He had to admit to himself that she was probably correct about his going to the Thompson farm and, reluctantly, he set about tidying the office, doing exactly what he was told.

'Now I'd say this was somethin' of an official visit,' said Jimmy Thompson, when the new sheriff dismounted and stepped on to the front porch of the Thompson homestead, carrying the poster with him. Barry Day did not say anything as he handed Jimmy Thompson the poster, who simply glanced at it, laughed and handed it back. 'So what're you goin' to do about it?' he challenged. 'That was a few years ago now, I doubt if there's anyone left who even remembers it.'

'As I see it, it doesn't matter who remembers,' said Barry. 'It's my duty to arrest you in the first place, after that it's up to the lawyers and the judges.'

'Five hundred dollars must be an awful lot of money to a young feller like you,' grinned Thompson. 'Anyhow, you can't collect since you can't even legally arrest me.'

'This badge gives me that authority,' said Barry, thrusting his chest out to show his badge of office. 'I've been appointed quite properly.'

'I don't doubt it, young feller!' laughed Thompson. 'An' I must give you credit for havin' the guts to come out here an' try to arrest me. There's just one small problem, a problem even the last sheriff discovered he couldn't do anythin' about. This territory ain't in the Union so federal laws don't automatically apply an' arrestin' a man for a crime committed in another part of the country is one of 'em. If I'd murdered the guy, they might've been able to get a warrant to have me what they call, extradited, or somethin', but even that ain't no guarantee.'

Barry Day was suddenly very uncertain of his ground. When he had decided to assert what he thought was his legal duty, the idea of the territory being outside the Union and therefore beyond federal law had never entered his head. Of course, he did know that they were not part of the Union but it had never seemed to matter in the past. 'I think you ought to come back to town with me an' we'll sort it out/ there,' he said. 'I've got me some legal books back at the office an' I'm sure

Mr Brown will probably know more about it than I do.'

'Tell you what,' grinned Thompson. 'You go back an' check your facts; I know you'll find I'm right. If I ain't, you just come right back an' take me in. I can't say fairer'n that, can I?'

Jimmy Thompson seemed so certain of his facts that Barry felt that he had just made a fool of himself. Brogan had warned against rushing in but he had thought that he knew better. Now he sensed that it was the badge on his chest which was talking and not reason. Three of the brothers, Wilbur—his arm in a sling—Amos and Johnny and one of the sisters, Betty, came out on to the porch and looked enquiringly at their father, who waved his hand, laughed and left them.

'That badge ain't goin' to protect you,' said Wilbur. 'You just remember that it don't pay to mess about with a Thompson.'

'And you remember that I'm sheriff

around these parts,' said Barry. 'You don't frighten me an' provided you don't cause no trouble, you won't get treated no different from nobody else.'

'I guess you'll be gettin' wed a mite sooner than you'd planned,' smiled Betty, sidling up to him. 'I reckon you should change your mind an' get rid of that harridan Mary Tranter. I always had a fancy for you myself, still have as a matter of fact. You marry me instead an' I reckon you can say that you'll be the most powerful sheriff this territory ever had. There'd be nobody dare to oppose you, not with the backin' of the Thompsons.' She slipped her arms around his neck and pressed herself close to him. 'Now if'n you was wantin' proof that everythin' would be OK, all I have to do is give the nod to my brothers here an' you an' me will have the house to ourselves for the next couple of hours. How about it?' There were undisguised sniggers from the brothers.

'I've got me better things to do with my time,' said Barry, slightly nervous. 'Anyhow, I like to know where my woman has been.'

She suddenly stepped back and brought the flat of her hand hard across his face. 'You sayin' I'm dirty!' she exploded. 'You take that remark back or else I'll tell Wilbur to kill you.'

'I just said that I like to know where my woman has been,' said Barry, stepping back beyond the range of her hand. 'I wouldn't advise doin' nothin' stupid like killin' me; I am a sheriff now an' the law don't take too kindly to havin' sheriffs murdered.'

'You'd better get out while you still can,' snarled Amos. 'You ain't got that saddletramp to hold your hand now.'

At that moment Jimmy Thompson returned carrying a letter which he handed to the sheriff. 'Wasn't sure if I still had it,' he said. 'That's from a lawyer in Cherokee Springs. He quotes some part of the law which says that the only way I can be taken back for trial is if I do it voluntarily.'

'Can I keep this?' asked Barry.

'No, sir,' said Thompson. 'Things have a habit of goin' missin' in this town. I used to own a lot of property hereabouts, but I can't prove a thing since all the deeds have disappeared. It was before your time, son, at least before you started wearin' long pants, but certain folk took over what was rightly mine an' the deeds an' things suddenly disappeared so I couldn't do a damned thing about it. Ever since then me an' most of the folk in Riverdale have been at war an' that's the way things is goin' to stay until I find out what happened.'

'If there has been anything illegal,' said Barry, thinking about the documents they had found, 'I can assure you that I shall look into it and if you are right, I shall see to it that your property is restored to you.'

Jimmy Thompson laughed loudly. 'Fine words, son, fine words an' I've heard 'em all before. I really believe that you mean what you say as well. The pity is that you won't be allowed to see it through. Mark my words, Sheriff, you talk about it to folk like Chas Brown an' he'll soon find a way to get rid of you. Why do you think the last sheriff left town? He was on to somethin', I know. He was a fair-minded man, but suddenly he disappeared. They reckon he just packed his bags and rode out of town but did he really? I reckon he's buried out there somewheres.'

'That's a serious charge, Mr Thompson,' said Barry.

'And one I mean,' asserted Thompson. 'They say it was me who drove him out, but I know it wasn't, it was Chas Brown.'

'At least you've given me somethin' to think about,' said Barry.

'An' this is somethin' else to think about,' said Thompson. 'If I was you I'd steer clear of anythin' that happens between me and that bum, McNally. He killed my son an' he's got to pay for it. If the law can't or won't do anythin', I will.'

'Murder is still murder even if this territory isn't part of the Union, Mr Thompson,' said Barry. 'Your son was killed as he tried to murder Silas Morgan; I saw it happen. If you kill Mr McNally, in anythin' but a fair fight, I'll have to charge you with murder and I do know that I won't need an out-of-state warrant for somethin' like that.'

'We'll see, son,' sneered Thompson, 'we'll see.'

'Just what do we do with these folders?' asked Brogan, indicating the three folders which seemed to have come from the bank. He had explained to Mary where they had been found.

'They must have been kept here for a purpose,' said Mary. 'They can go back in the cabinet until someone has the time to look through them. Most of this stuff is so old that it might as well be put in a pile in the back yard and burned.'

Brogan obediently put the folders back in the cabinet and began the task of carrying unwanted papers and material out into the yard, where it seemed to occupy a space twice as large as it had inside. Eventually Mary decided that everything that was of no value had been sorted and told Brogan to light the fire.

Chas Brown came across and wondered if they were doing the right thing or not and asked if they had discovered anything of importance. Mary showed him the poster relating to Jimmy Thompson and it was plain that the mayor already knew of it. Once again he asked if there had been anything else of importance and were they certain that what they were burning was not important, but by that time it was too late. Mary appeared to be about to tell Chas about the three files when Brogan casually touched her arm and shook his head slightly and he assured the mayor that what had been burned was out of date and worthless.

'You knew about Jimmy Thompson being wanted for assault and robbery?' said Mary. 'Why hasn't anything been done about it before now?'

'Before now?' queried Chas.

'Barry has gone out to the Thompsons,' she said. 'We think he went to arrest Jimmy Thompson.'

Chas Brown laughed. 'I suppose he has to learn.'

'Meaning what?' asked Brogan.

'I'll leave him to tell you,' said Chas, laughing again.

At a little after eleven o'clock, Barry returned and immediately became very agitated, demanding to know exactly what had been burned and for once Mary seemed to step back and give way.

'You could have destroyed some vital evidence!' complained Barry. 'I learnt me a thing or two out at the Thompson place, even if I couldn't arrest him.' He explained about not being in the Union but he did not say anything about the suggestion by Jimmy Thompson that he had been cheated out of property or that the previous sheriff might have been murdered. 'Those files!' he almost screamed. 'The ones that looked like they came from the bank, you haven't burnt those have you?'

'Relax,' said Brogan, 'they're all in the cabinet. What's so hell-fire suddenly important about them?'

'I don't think you'd understand or appreciate, Brogan,' said Barry. 'Sorry, I can't tell you a thing, not yet, mainly because I don't know for certain myself. The one thing I must ask you not to do is tell anyone about them, nobody, not even your father,' he said to Mary, 'and definitely not Chas Brown. You must promise.'

'Of course we promise,' said Mary. 'But it would help if we knew what this was all about.'

'I need to check on a few things first,' said Barry.

'I don't know what this is all about,' said Brogan, 'an' frankly I don't want to know, but the mayor was here just before you came back an' he seemed mighty interested in knowin' if any important documents had been found.'

'Did you tell him about those files?' asked Barry, quite concerned.

'Nope,' replied Brogan. 'Son, this is all gettin' too complicated for the likes of me. I never did have me any schoolin' but I taught myself to read an' write an' I'm pretty good with figures but all this legal stuff is beyond me.'

'You can't keep it to yourself,' said Mary. 'You have to trust someone and if you can't trust either me or Mr McNally, who can you trust?'

The sheriff flopped into a chair and stared at the floor for a short time before retrieving the files from the cabinet. He slowly turned over each sheet of paper, grunting occasionally and stopping to read something more closely. Eventually he placed the files on the desk and put his fingertips together and whistled softly.

'If what I read is what I think it is,' he said at length, 'then I ain't surprised at Chas Brown wantin' to know if we'd found anythin' important. The state this office was in it seems obvious to me that someone else searched it, probably when the last sheriff left and it seems they didn't find what they were looking for but we have.'

'Barry!' said Mary, firmly. 'Unless we know just what you're talking about, how are we expected to help you?'

'I reckon it's none of my business,' said Brogan. 'If you like, I'll go take a walk round the town while you two talk.'

'No need for that,' said Barry. 'OK, I suppose three heads are better than one and I'm not so certain I know what's been going on myself ...' He proceeded to tell them about what had happened and what had been claimed by Jimmy Thompson at the Thompson farm.

'You've got yourself a problem, young feller,' said Brogan, when the sheriff had told his story. 'I said sheriffin' wasn't goin' to be easy. All I can say is that you need the help of a good lawyer or someone from the governor's office. I wouldn't trust that kind of information to a local lawyer.'

'We don't have one,' said Barry. 'We haven't had one since James McBurney died. You're right, I need to take all this to the governor, but what do I tell the mayor, he's sure to want to know what business I have there?'

'I remember Jimmy Thompson sayin' somethin' about the town owin' him,' said Brogan, 'but I've heard that kind of talk before an' it don't usually amount to that much.'

Mary had been looking through the files and looked up. 'Barry's right,' she said. 'Even I can see that something is very wrong even by flicking through these. It looks like Jimmy Thompson was cheated out of quite a lot of property, but that's just an impression, it would have to be sorted out properly by the lawyers.'

'What about the last sheriff bein' murdered?' asked Brogan. 'Could there be anythin' in that?'

'Maybe,' shrugged Barry. 'The fact that these files were deliberately hidden makes it look like he was on to something and it never was really explained why he left Riverdale so suddenly. I don't suppose we'll ever know the truth of that though, it was three years ago and if he was murdered I have no doubt that his body was well hidden. No, I don't think there would be much point in following that line. The thing is, I need to get these files and all the information I have to the governor and it might be difficult explaining to Mr Brown just why I need to go.'

'Then let me take them,' suggested

Mary. 'I have the perfect excuse ...' Both men looked at her questioningly. 'Our wedding is being brought forward so I have to go and buy a few things; after all, a girl can't be expected to turn up at her own wedding in any shabby old dress, can she? I also have the advantage of knowing the governor personally. I could even say I was inviting him to the wedding.'

'There's your answer,' said Brogan. 'It looks like you've got things sorted out pretty well between you. You don't need me any more so I guess I'll just saddle up an' be on my way.'

'Don't forget Jimmy Thompson,' reminded Barry. 'He told me to keep out of anything between you and him, he still seems determined to kill you for shooting Frank.'

'The best thing you can do, Mr McNally,' said Mary, 'is ride on as soon as you can. I know Jimmy Thompson said that you would be followed and killed, but at least you would stand a chance.'

'Meaning that I don't stand a chance the way things are,' said Brogan. 'Ma'am, I ain't never turned tail on a fight yet an' I'm too old to start now. I don't go lookin' for trouble but when it comes up on me I ain't afraid to face it.'

'I thought you said the best thing you could do was to saddle up and be on your way,' reminded Mary.

'That was until you went on about Jimmy Thompson,' said Brogan. 'Anyhow, I did promise your young feller I would teach him how to shoot an' believe me, he needs to know, especially against a man like Thompson and his sons. If I know someone like Jimmy Thompson, he's taught his sons pretty well too.'

'You are just plain pig-headed,' smiled Mary. 'But I'm glad; you're right, he does need some tuition.'

'Don't know for sure what tuition means,' grinned Brogan, 'but he sure has some learnin' to do.'

'Good!' she beamed. 'Now, Barry, you write out everything you know and I'll take it and the files to the governor the day after tomorrow. If you need any help with explaining things, let me know and I'll help you to write it properly.'

'In the meantime,' said Brogan, 'I reckon we'd best get out there an' waste a few more bullets until you can hit somethin' properly.'

'I might be the sheriff round here,' grinned Barry, 'but it looks like even I have to do as I'm told. OK. OK. You can both have things your way. Right now, Brogan, you and me had better go an practise. Mary, you can come round here this evening and we'll sort out what I have to say to the governor. If anyone wants to know what we're doin', we can say we're still sortin' out the mess in the office.'

'Or we can tell them to go to hell and mind their own business!' laughed Mary.

179

EIGHT

Brogan had been very patient with Barry for almost three hours the previous afternoon, but he felt that his persistence had been rewarded in that the sheriff could now shoot reasonably straight and had even managed to hit a small, moving target several times. The speed of his draw was still rather slow and would need a lot more time spent on it, more time than Brogan was prepared to give. His accuracy with a rifle was about what Brogan expected and all that was needed was time. Most farmers and ranchers were usually fairly accurate with a shotgun or a rifle but very few could use a handgun with any reasonable degree of efficiency, although under normal circumstances they had very little need for such a weapon since their main enemy was usually vermin in one form or another. The result was that most did not even own a handgun or if they did it was usually some ancient relic. Besides, handguns were very expensive and farmers were a very thrifty lot and would not waste money on something they were hardly ever likely to need or use.

For his part, Barry Day felt very satisfied with his progress and in some ways was perhaps a little too complacent, imagining that he was more advanced than he really was, something Brogan warned him against, telling him that he should always approach any confrontation with the assumption that the other man was better and faster than he was. Barry promised to keep that advice in mind.

Saturday was the one day of the week when Riverdale really came to life, the day when whole families descended on the town from the outlying farms both to sell their produce and to buy those items they needed. Most of the morning and a large part of the main street was taken up in a market atmosphere and by midday most of the trading had been completed and the men drifted off to the saloon. The women gathered in small groups in houses or stores, gossiping and pulling to pieces anyone unfortunate enough not to be in their particular group.

For the first time, Barry Day paraded himself and his badge of office throughout the town, intervening in a couple of disputes and evicting one particularly noisy and offensive drunk from the saloon, something which would previously have been done very efficiently by Mick Fletcher, but he seemed quite happy to allow the new sheriff to assert his authority. The vast majority of people appeared pleased that at last Riverdale had a sheriff and seemed to accept his authority without question. Brogan had offered to accompany Barry on his rounds, but this had been refused.

'You won't be around to hold my hand much longer,' said Barry. 'The folk of this town will have to come to terms with the fact that I am the sheriff whether they like it or not. Anyhow, if you were with me I could never be certain if it was me or you who made them toe the line.' In a way, Brogan was pleased not to have to accompany the sheriff and agreed that he had to show his own authority.

Just before Barry started on his patrol of the town, Chas Brown, the mayor, came into the office and noted that he hardly recognized the place. 'Did you find anything of importance?' he asked, repeating his question of the previous day. 'I always intended to have the place cleaned out but somehow I never got round to it.'

'Well it sure looked like somebody had been searchin' for somethin',' said Barry, giving a knowing look at Brogan. 'All we found was a Wanted poster for Jimmy Thompson.'

'Kids, I know some did break in once a few months ago,' smiled Chas. 'So I gather you rode out to see Thompson, I also imagine that you found out why nothing had been done about it.'

'I could've saved myself a lot of bother if someone had told me beforehand,' said Barry.

'And I suppose he fed you the line about him once owning a lot of property in the area,' continued Chas. Barry nodded, there did not seem to be a lot of point in denying it. 'It's true, he did,' smiled Chas, 'but he either lost it gamblin'—he used to be a very heavy gambler—or he sold it because he needed the money. I expect he told you that he had been cheated out of it, he trots out that line quite regularly.'

The idea that Jimmy Thompson had been a heavy gambler did not ring true with Brogan; Jimmy was too much like he was and, in his experience, men such as he and Jimmy did not gamble, they might take calculated risks but they never gambled, either in the sense of gaming or with their lives. He had met many men

184

who had lost property and fortunes at the gaming tables but they had always admitted the fact, sometimes blaming themselves or sometimes accusing others of conspiring to cheat them, but none had ever denied gambling and as far as he knew, Jimmy Thompson had not mentioned the fact, seemingly being more concerned that documents had been either forged or altered, a claim which even on a brief examination by inexperienced people like himself, Barry and Mary appeared to have some substance.

When the mayor had returned to his store, Brogan asked Barry to question Jimmy Thompson if he had the opportunity asking him specifically about the gambling. Barry had a better idea, he would broach the subject with those men whom he knew were gamblers, although the really big-time gamblers had long since departed, at about the time a minor gold rush had died when it was discovered that the lucky strike which had started it had proved nothing more than a one off. A few had made some money from the gold and quickly departed on rumours of other and richer strikes, but most had ended up financially worse off than when they had started.

The Thompsons, too, usually came into town on a Saturday to sell and buy just like everyone else, and this Saturday was no exception, despite the presence of Brogan. The only ones missing were Carl and, surprisingly according to nearly everyone, Jimmy himself. The excuse given by the four women—Jane, with her arm in a sling—was that someone had to stay behind and look after Carl. It was noticeable that the brothers took no active part in either the selling or buying and were apparently not expected to, other than to lug a few sacks about. After that they were seemingly more intent on seeing which of them could drink the most beer in the shortest time.

Brogan deliberately chose to keep out of the way, partly because there were just too many people about for his liking and partly because he did not want his presence to provoke any trouble between himself and the Thompsons. It did appear that the Thompsons were not too anxious to confront Brogan either. Whether this was because of a natural wariness or perhaps because Jimmy had ordered that they should keep out of trouble was unclear. What was very noticeable, according to Barry Day on one of his regular visits to the office, was that none of the Thompsons was wearing a gun and although the brothers were very rowdy in the saloon, they had not caused any problems yet.

It also seemed that Saturday was the day when a barber made an appearance in Riverdale. He actually turned out to be one of the farmers who had been a barber before taking up farming, and was doing a steady trade throughout the morning on the boardwalk outside the saloon. Brogan stroked his hair and decided that it was about time he had his hair cut, but he waited until almost midday before venturing out of the office.

'You're that saddlebum what's been causin' all the trouble, ain't you?' said the barber as he started to clip away at Brogan's dirty hair.

'So I'm told,' said Brogan. 'I didn't see it that way though.'

'Don't suppose you did,' muttered the barber. 'That's the trouble with folk like you, you don't appreciate how others feel or what the background is. That was a dumb thing to do, kill young Frank.'

'Dumb for who?' asked Brogan.

'All of us,' said the barber. 'More for us than for you. You'll either end up dead or you'll ride out an' leave someone else to sort out the mess.'

'You've got a new sheriff,' Brogan pointed out. The reply was a sardonic laugh. 'Have you known Jimmy Thompson long?' continued Brogan. 'I hear he was quite a gambler in his time.' This comment brought another sardonic laugh.

188

'Don't know where you heard that,' said the barber. 'I've known him almost all my life an' his an' I don't even remember him with a card in his hand.' He brushed some loose hair off Brogan's shoulders and held out his hand. 'Twenty-five cents,' he said. Brogan paid up thinking that twenty-five cents was a little on the expensive side. However, he felt that he had established that Jimmy Thompson was not a gambler. This was confirmed later when Barry said that his talking to the regular gamblers had indicated that none of the Thompsons, not even the brothers, were or ever had been gamblers. The nearest the brothers ever came to gambling was a few hands between themselves for pennies.

The activities of the morning may have passed off without any incidents, but the afternoon produced two problems. The first was when Silas Morgan came rushing into the office looking for the sheriff but who appeared satisfied finding only Brogan.

'It's Billy,' he wheezed. 'I can't find him nowheres an' the last I saw of him was about ten o'clock this mornin'. Me an' Walter have searched the whole town but we can't find him.'

'So what do you expect the sheriff to do about it?' asked Brogan. 'He's got his work cut out keepin' law an' order.'

'An' doin' a pretty good job of it too,' admitted the old man. 'This is the first time Billy has gone missin' for so long,' he went on. 'You know what he's like, he's more of a danger to himself than anyone else. I've asked practically everyone in town but nobody's seen him. It ain't like him to go off like that.'

'So what do you want me or the sheriff to do?' asked Brogan again.

'Organize a search party,' replied Silas.

'That's somethin' you'd better ask the sheriff about,' said Brogan. However, he could see that the old man was very worried and in a way he felt that he owed both him and Walter Morgan something.

'Tell you what,' he said. 'I'll get out there an' do a bit of lookin' about myself, I can't say fairer'n that.'

'I'd sure appreciate that,' said Silas. 'I'll carry on lookin' as well. Walter's got too much work on; Saturday is always his busiest day.' Brogan was tempted to say that he had nothing better to do and was becoming rather bored but he resisted, not wishing to offend the old man.

Silas left the office and Brogan was just about to lock the door and go and find the sheriff when the second problem of the afternoon reared its head in the form of Barry Day suddenly appearing on the boardwalk outside the office prodding Amos Thompson ahead of him.

'I warned him!' said the sheriff, forcing Amos through the office and pushing him into one of the four cells. 'I warned him,' he repeated, as he locked the cell. 'He was makin' life hell for one of the Sanderson girls. She's accused him of attempted rape, but I don't think that one's goin' to stick, not with her reputation, but even she has a right not to be pestered. I warned him after she'd complained to me, but he just laughed and ignored me, tellin' me I wasn't a proper sheriff. Then he went an' grabbed at her again, so I arrested him.'

'Probably the best thing you could do,' agreed Brogan. 'By the way, I was just comin' out to look for you. Silas Morgan has just been in to say that Billy has gone missin'. I said I'd take a look about to see if I could find him, I sure ain't got nothin' else to do.'

'Yeh, I heard he was askin' about,' said Barry. 'I'd appreciate it if you did take a look. More'n likely he's taken himself off an' hid somewhere. Billy don't really like too many folk around him.'

'I know how he feels!' grinned Brogan. He left the office not knowing where to start looking, but he could see Silas up at the far end of town and decided that he would start his search down by the river.

As was apparently quite normal on Saturdays, most of the children had left their parents to do whatever work there was and had congregated at the river, many of them using the bridge, which was about ten feet above the water, to dive off, fully clothed. Brogan shuddered at the thought that anyone should submerge themselves in water for the pleasure of it. He even noted that one or two of the older boys and girls were among the trees indulging in certain activities of which the parents of the girls would almost certainly not have approved.

'Have any of you kids seen Billy Morgan?' he asked the group sitting on the bank.

'Daft Billy?' asked a boy. 'Sure we seen him. We seen him this mornin'.'

'Which way did he go?' asked Brogan.

'Downstream I reckon,' grinned the boy.

'Downstream?' queried Brogan.

'Sure,' laughed one of the girls, 'he'd got himself into a punt somehow. I remember someone untyin' it an' Daft Billy was took away downriver.'

'When was this?' asked Brogan.

'Oh, maybe sometime after ten,' replied the boy.

'Didn't you tell anybody?' sighed Brogan.

'What for?' asked the girl in a matter-of-fact way. 'It ain't no concern of ours what Daft Billy does. My ma has allus said I was to have nothin' at all to do with him, she reckoned whatever was wrong with him was probably catchin'.'

'Mine too,' agreed the boy. 'Nobody had anythin' to do with Daft Billy, we know he could set the Devil after us if he wanted. The last preacher in Riverdale told us that, he reckoned Billy's real father was the Devil.' Brogan was not really surprised, he had met a good many priests and preachers who had been very intolerant of people with defects such as Billy.

'Well thanks anyhow,' sighed Brogan. At least he had been able to establish in a very short time what had happened to

Billy which was more than his grandfather had been able to, but then he thought that probably most people just did not want to involve themselves. Not having any knowledge of what the river was like further downstream or how far the punt was likely to have travelled, Brogan decided to return to the sheriff's office and tell Barry. If anyone could organize a search party it would be the new sheriff. However, it was very apparent that the sheriff was having a few problems of his own.

A large crowd had gathered outside the jail, although it was plain that all were there purely as onlookers. The focus of their attention was the four Thompson women and five Thompson brothers, all the brothers now armed, standing in front of the office shouting, threatening and demanding the release of the sixth brother, Amos, from the jail. Barry Day was standing at the open door, unwisely Brogan thought, his rifle held across his chest ready for action.

'You ain't got no cause to hold a Thompson,' shouted one of the brothers. 'All you got is the word of that slut Maggie Sanderson ...'

'Who the hell are you callin' a slut?' demanded a male voice from the crowd.

'Your Maggie!' barked the brother. 'Everybody knows what she is. There can't be a man in Riverdale an' more'n one passin' stranger who she ain't spread her legs to. She's only complainin' 'cos Amos wouldn't have nothin' to do with her.'

'You take that back!' shouted the man. 'You take that back or you'll have me to deal with ...' It was very noticeable that the man did not leave the safety of the crowd, especially when invited to do so by the brother.

'That ain't what happened,' said Barry Day from the doorway. 'I gave Amos fair warnin' but he took no heed. Maggie Sanderson has just as much right to protection as anyone else. You want him out of jail it's goin' to cost you a ten-dollar fine for a breach of the peace. You pay up an' he can go free.'

'Damn you an' your ten dollars,' hissed Mrs Thompson. 'No Thompson has ever paid a fine an' no Thompson ever will. If you don't let him out in the next five minutes I'll order my boys to break in an' let him out.'

'Over my dead body!' said Barry, taking a tighter grip on his rifle and spreading his legs a little wider apart.

'That can be arranged!' snarled out Mother Thompson.

'I don't think you quite understood what the sheriff was saying,' said Brogan, as he stepped through the crowd. 'If I heard correctly, he said somethin' about a ten-dollar fine for a breach of the peace.'

'An' just what the hell has it got to do with you?' snarled Wilbur Thompson. 'This ain't none of your business, McNally.'

'It would appear that I've just made it my business,' replied Brogan. He stood alongside Barry, his rifle held deceptively casually in one hand and his other hand poised close to his holster.

The almost frivolous mood amongst the crowd had suddenly changed and all sensed imminent danger and withdrew beyond what they thought was the range of any stray bullets. The Thompsons were left on their own in the street opposite the jail, all beginning to look nervously about and finger their guns but none apparently prepared to make the first move against a man whom they knew to be very fast and very accurate.

Brogan had seen Mayor Chas Brown on the fringe of the crowd and he called out to him. 'You're the mayor, Mr Brown,' he called. 'What should your sheriff do with Amos Thompson? You have to remember that if you don't back him you might as well take the badge off him right now.'

'I ... er ...' faltered Chas. 'It must be a matter for the sheriff, I can't interfere in matters of law.'

'Are you sure you're on safe ground?' Brogan whispered through the side of his mouth to the sheriff.

'Hanged if I know,' Barry whispered in reply. 'I don't even know if I can charge him with anythin' an' I said ten dollars right off the top of my head.'

'Then you'd better stick to it,' hissed Brogan.

'Amos stays where he is until either he or one of you pays up ten dollars,' said Barry, out loud. 'After that there'll be a further two dollar a day charge for food.' He whispered to Brogan. 'I just thought of that one as well.'

'You're learnin' fast,' grinned Brogan.

'Now what was that about you orderin' your boys to break into the jail?' Barry challenged Mother Thompson.

'You won't have that saddlebum to be a nursemaid for ever,' she growled in response. 'I'm surprised you ain't made a run for it before now,' she said to Brogan. 'I reckon you must want to die.'

'It seems to me that you Thompsons are all talk,' grinned Brogan. 'All I've heard these past few days is talk about killin' me but so far not one of you has been able to put your words into actions. What's so different this time? You just pay up the ten dollars right now an' Amos can go free. If you don't wanna pay up, just remember it's goin' to cost an extra two dollars a day.'

Mother Thompson used a lot of invective and words which even Brogan was surprised to hear from any woman, but, eventually, she pulled a wad of money from her apron pocket, peeled off a ten dollar bill, crumpled it up and threw it on to the boardwalk by the office door. The sheriff picked it up, straightened it out and nodded. Without another word he went into the office, unlocked the cell and allowed Amos to walk free. There had been a buzz of excitement when Mother Thompson had paid up, but most wondered if she would have done so had the saddletramp not been there. However, it was still a much talked about victory over the Thompsons.

Far from being pleased to see her son, Mother Thompson immediately slapped Amos around the face and told him that he would have to pay her the ten dollars back and then she frog-marched him back to their wagon and they left town to jeers from a great many citizens. Brogan thought that the jeers probably hurt more than being forced to back down over the payment of the fine.

'Well done!' enthused Chas Brown, entering the office. 'I was, of course, going to advise you not to back down, but I thought it would be best if it came from you. Anyway, it did give you some experience. Now, I believe you have ten dollars which now belongs to town funds.'

'Five!' said Barry, making the mayor look sharply at him. 'I've just decided that you're payin' me such a lousy salary that

I get to take half of all fines.'

'You ... you can't do that!' exclaimed Chas.

'I just did,' smiled Barry. 'Since it was me who set the fine, I think it only right I should get a share. If you don't like it I'll set fines at about ten cents and no charge for meals. I reckon you'd soon complain about that.'

'But half!' gasped the mayor. 'I might agree to say, one fifth ...'

'Half!' insisted the sheriff. In the end, Chas Brown reluctantly agreed but returned to his store muttering to himself and smarting from having been put in his place by his young sheriff. Not only that, but he resented having to sign a receipt for the remaining five dollars. To be fair to everyone, Barry also signed a receipt for his five dollars.

'Just to show that everythin's above board,' he grinned. 'Now, did you find anythin' out about Billy Morgan? I didn't have time to talk to anyone, the Thompsons turned up just after you'd left.' Brogan told him what he had learned from the children and Barry nodded sagely. 'It's fairly slow, but deep for about five miles,' he said. 'After that it gets a bit shallower an' rocky in parts. Then there's Davis Rapids. He might have survived those but he sure wouldn't survive Granite Falls, that's a drop of about three hundred feet. I reckon if Billy is found, it'll only be his body.'

'Well somebody ought to at least go an' look for him,' said Brogan.

'It's Saturday!' sighed Barry. 'The first Saturday I've been sheriff an' if I know some of 'em round here, they'll all try to show me that me bein' sheriff ain't goin' to make no difference to them.'

'I'll take Silas an' Walter,' said Brogan. 'We shouldn't need anyone else an' if we do find the lad alive he'll be terrified, so faces he knows might be the only way to calm him.'

'I wish I could go myself,' said Barry,

'but frankly I don't think it would be wise. I wouldn't be surprised if the Thompsons don't hit town again and I need to be here to stop any trouble before it really starts.'

'Don't worry about it,' smiled Brogan. 'The three of us will manage fine.'

Brogan left the office and went straight to the smithy where Walter had just finished shoeing a horse. He explained the position and Walter immediately set about saddling his horse. Brogan too saddled his old horse, telling her that it was about time that she earned her keep and that she had had it too easy for the past few days. There were a couple of snorts of protest but she was soon saddled. Walter decided that it would be as well if Silas remained in town just in case Brogan's information turned out to be incorrect and Billy turned up after they had gone. Silas objected to being left behind but was persuaded that he needed to stay.

Brogan and Walter reached the bridge

where the story was confirmed by some other children, one claiming that his mother had been told but that she had said it might be the best thing that could happen to Billy.

'That, unfortunately, is what most folk think,' sighed Walter. 'I must admit that there have been times when I've thought so myself, but he is flesh and blood. Let's hope we're not too late.'

NINE

They discovered the punt—or what was left of it—below Davis Rapids. It had been holed through the bottom and had broken sides where it had been battered against the rocks, but there was no sign of Billy. Walter was quite convinced that his nephew had been drowned and was ready to abandon the search there and then, but Brogan was not so easily deterred or convinced and he immediately began a close search of the riverbank. However, after moving very slowly downstream for about a mile and finding nothing except a few animal tracks, he, too, began to think that perhaps his optimism was unfounded. The punt had been found on the side of the river they had followed and they had assumed that if Billy had survived he must have somehow made it to the nearest bank. Brogan decided to retrace their steps but this time on the opposite bank and crossed at a reasonably shallow part.

'I'd say he made it,' declared Brogan, pointing to a scrape in the bank. He dismounted to make a closer examination. 'Yes, it sure looks like this is where he managed to get out,' he said. Walter, too, dismounted and examined the scrape but he was not at all convinced.

'That looks as if it could've been made by almost anythin',' he said, looking about. They were surrounded by a forest, not dense, but reasonably thickly wooded. 'It could've easily been a bear or a wolf or even a deer,' he said.

'Like most folk, you see what you want to see,' said Brogan. 'Since when have bears or wolves worn boots?' He pointed to two marks in the clay. 'Boot heels,' he said. 'This is where he came out all right.'

'How the hell can you tell if they're boot marks?' asked Walter. 'They could be anythin' as far as I'm concerned.' Brogan stood up and set his own heel in the clay alongside one of the marks. Walter looked at both prints and almost reluctantly appeared to be convinced.

'Now we look for which way he went,' said Brogan. 'Someone like Billy should be easy to follow. I only hope we find him before nightfall; he's wet an' it gets pretty damned cold at night.'

As predicted, there was no shortage of signs although Brogan was surprised at just how much progress had been made by someone who was as badly crippled as Billy apparently was. About an hour later Brogan nudged Walter.

'There's wolves up ahead,' he said. 'Probably they've either made a kill or found a carcass.'

'Billy!' croaked Walter. 'It must be Billy.'

'Naw,' assured Brogan. 'Probably a deer.'

'How the hell do you know that?' demanded Walter. 'I hear tell of folk bein' attacked by wolves in these forests.'

'Wolves don't attack humans,' said Brogan. 'I ain't met nobody yet who's actually seen it happen. It's always somethin' they hear from other folk who have heard. I seen plenty of wolves, starvin' wolves too, an' while they might attack to get at a man's horse or mule, they always leave the man alone. I ain't never heard of 'em eatin' a dead man either. Foxes now, they is different, they don't attack but they ain't so fussy about what they eat.'

'I'll take your word for it,' said Walter, not convinced and still quite certain that they were going to find the remains of his nephew. 'Anyhow, how the hell do you know there's wolves up ahead?'

'I can sense 'em, hear 'em an' taste 'em,' replied Brogan. This was no boasting on his part, he really could smell them and even taste them; it was just one of those things he had been conditioned to over many years. Naturally enough, Walter did not believe that any man could know these things, but his scepticism evaporated somewhat when they saw the wolves in a clearing, gathered round a carcass which was plainly a deer.

The animals had sensed the approach of the two men even before they had appeared, in much the same way that Brogan had detected them and very slowly and resentfully moved to one side as the men approached. Walter had his rifle at the ready but Brogan did not appear too concerned as they rode past. The wolves closed in the instant they were a safe distance away.

'Bears!' said Brogan suddenly. 'Now they'll attack a man an' I do know they've been known to eat human flesh. I once found a body with an arm missin'. I found it a while later bein' chewed at by a big grizzly. You can't always tell though, sometimes they'll turn tail an' run as soon as they see you, sometimes they'll just carry on as if you weren't there, an' sometimes they'll charge at first sight, especially a female who has a cub somewheres nearby.'

'The trouble with Billy is he ain't got no sense of fear or danger,' said Walter. 'He's liable to just walk straight up to a wolf or a bear.'

'Then let's hope he hasn't met any,' said Brogan.

By that time the light was fading rapidly and Brogan said that if they had not found him within the next half-hour they would have to call off the search for the night.

Half an hour later, although they had come across some tracks which were plainly not of animal origin, they settled by a small stream for the night. Brogan managed to shoot a large bird and he also found some bulbs and, although Walter was very uncertain about eating the bulbs, he did appreciate the bird.

'Listen!' said Brogan, shaking Walter. They had been asleep for about two hours when Brogan suddenly sat up and listened hard. 'That noise wasn't made by no animal.'

'I don't hear a thing,' said Walter.

'I don't now,' admitted Brogan, 'but I heard what sounded like a cry, pretty close as well.' He listened again and this time there was another cry. 'There it goes again,' he said. 'You must've heard it that time.'

'I heard it,' confirmed Walter. 'It could've been anythin' as far as I'm concerned.'

'Well, it sure wasn't no wolf or bear,'

said Brogan. 'An' it sure wasn't no animal I ever heard before.'

'I don't know how the hell you can tell the difference,' grumbled Walter. 'OK, I'll take your word for it, but what the hell can we do about it tonight? Just look about, you can hardly see a hand in front of you.'

'There's not a lot we can do until it gets light,' admitted Brogan, 'but it came from over there.' He pointed to his right. 'Have you any idea what's over there?'

'Not the faintest,' said Walter. 'I've lived in these parts almost all my life but this is the first time I've been out here. All I know is we can't be too far from the Thompsons farm, but I don't know just how far.'

Brogan nodded and settled down again, but this time listening out for the cry which he heard two or three times more which in turn helped him to pinpoint exactly where it was coming from.

At first light both men were on their way,

Brogan quite certain of where he was going and it was less then ten minutes later that they found themselves at the top of a sheer cliff of about 200 feet in height.

The cries had stopped about half an hour after they had heard the first one and so far they had not heard any others, although Brogan's senses told him that they had found Billy. He could not explain his feelings to Walter and, knowing that he would not be believed if he did, he did not try.

Both men peered over the edge of the cliff and at first neither of them could see nor hear anything unusual. Slightly to their right the drop was not completely sheer; there was a rock scree but it was certainly too steep and too loose to consider going down, even on foot. One slip would have sent either one of them crashing to their deaths. Suddenly, however, Brogan grabbed Walter's arm and pointed.

'There he is!' he said. Walter looked hard but apparently could not see anything.

'About halfway down, a few yards to the left of the scree,' continued Brogan. 'There's a ledge an' unless I'm seein' things, that's Billy lyin' there.'

Walter looked again and finally nodded. 'I see him,' he said. 'It sure looks like Billy but he don't seem to be movin'.'

'It's impossible to tell if he's alive or not,' said Brogan. He grabbed Walter's arm again as he was about to shout out. 'Don't call him!' he ordered. 'That's a narrow ledge an' if he recognizes your voice he might do somethin' stupid like tryin' to climb up an' that could be fatal.' He looked about for a way down, but other than the scree there was no way. 'We need a rope,' he said. 'I've got one on my saddle but it ain't long enough to get that far down, it must be at least a hundred feet. You have to get back to town an' get a longer rope an' some help.'

'The Thompson farm is nearer,' said Walter, 'but I guess you don't want me to go there.'

'I don't care where you go!' said Brogan, harshly. 'It's Billy what's important, not me. OK, you ride back to the Thompsons; I'll stay here an' keep an eye on things.' He looked down again. 'He's alive,' he said, 'I've just seen his leg move. Get goin', there's no time to waste, he might try climbin' an' there's no way of knowin' which way he'll go'. Walter lost no time, running to his horse and, for such a big man, leaping very agilely into the saddle. A few minutes later all sight and sound of him had disappeared.

'Bear Creek Canyon!' announced Jimmy Thompson. 'You say he's halfway down? How the hell did he get down there?'

'How doesn't matter,' said Walter. 'The fact is he's down there. Right now Brogan McNally is keepin' watch on him.'

'McNally!' said Jimmy. 'That saddlebum seems to get everywhere. If he's helpin' you I don't see why you need any help.'

'Well we do,' said Walter. 'OK, so

you an' McNally have a problem with each other, but Billy ain't part of that problem.'

'It was him what started it!' growled one of the brothers.

'Look,' gasped Walter, 'I don't care who started what, when or how. Right now I'm askin' you ... no ... I'm beggin' you for help. Just get Billy out of there an' then you an' McNally can sort out your own differences.'

'I don't see why we should even bother to help Billy,' said another brother. 'He might be better off dead.'

'OK, OK,' sighed Walter, 'I guess I'll just have to ride back to town an' get someone who is prepared to help.'

'I never said we wouldn't help,' said Jimmy. 'I guess we've all got our opinions about Billy, but I guess he can't help bein' the way he is, it's just that it sticks in my craw to have to work with that bastard McNally.'

'There's times when we all have to

swallow hard,' said Walter. 'Now do I ride back to town or not?'

'They'll go with you,' announced Mother Thompson as she came out on to the porch. 'I heard what you wanted an' I know what I'd expect as a mother. Jimmy, you just take the boys an' you go an' get that poor boy back up safely. If you're goin' to do anythin' about McNally then you can see to it after Billy is safe. Do you hear me?'

'I hear you, Ma,' nodded Jimmy. 'OK, Amos, you go get the buckboard, we might need it if Billy is hurt bad. The rest of you, saddle up, I'll go find a length of rope. I should have some long enough somewheres.'

'I thank you, Mrs Thompson,' said Walter, 'an' I know Billy would want to thank you too, if he could.'

'No thanks needed,' said Mother Thompson. 'You just make sure he don't go wanderin' off again.'

'He didn't wander off,' said Walter. 'He somehow got himself into a punt an' some of the kids pushed him out into the river.'

'That's kids these days!' said Mother Thompson. 'They ain't got no consideration.'

Ten minutes later, with Amos driving the buckboard, five other brothers, Jimmy Thompson and Walter started back to Bear Creek Canyon.

Jimmy Thompson and Brogan eyed each other warily as Brogan showed them just where Billy was lying and for a few moments the brothers and Walter thought that one of them was going to try and push the other over the edge.

'He's still alive,' said Brogan. 'His leg keeps movin'.'

'How the hell did he get down there?' asked Jimmy. 'He must have the Devil lookin' after him, just like that preacher used to say, anyone else would've fallen all the way an' been killed.'

'I was lookin' at that,' said Brogan. He

pointed to the scree. 'If I ain't mistaken he slid down there—see that line of freshly loosened stones? He was damned lucky, if he'd gone over a yard either side he would've been killed for sure. That was just about the only line which would taken him to that ledge.'

'OK,' said Jimmy, 'So we're here now an' just for the moment I'll forget just who you are, McNally. Who's goin' down there?'

'I will,' volunteered Brogan.

'Suit yourself,' Jimmy shrugged. 'I can send one of the boys down if you want, you an' me ain't young fellers like they are.'

'I'll do it,' said Brogan. 'I don't mean no disrespect to either you or your boys, but if he sees any of them he might just panic, he's more used to havin' 'em shoot at his feet. It's no use expectin' Walter to go down, he's one hell of a weight to haul back up.'

'That he is,' agreed Jimmy, 'an' I take your point about the boys. OK, let's get this rope tied round your chest an' start lowerin' you.'

'I hope you have strong hands,' said Brogan, grinning weakly. He was not normally afraid of anything but he had never been too happy scaling cliffs. He was not too worried about being allowed to fall, that understanding look had passed between the pair of them again.

Five minutes later, the rope was securely tied around Brogan's chest and, with four of the brothers taking the strain and slowly feeding out the rope, Brogan gingerly lowered himself over the edge, using the scree at first, but it very quickly became obvious that in doing so he was causing rock to fall which was crashing on to the ledge dangerously close to where Billy lay so he had to swing over to the clear cliff face.

It took longer to descend than Brogan had anticipated, about ten minutes in all but, on Jimmy's instruction, the rope was played out very slowly just in case any faster would have created a momentum they could not control. Eventually Brogan felt the narrow ledge under his feet and called out that he was down.

The ledge proved even narrower than it had appeared from the top and again Billy appeared to have the luck of the Devil with him since he had found the one wide spot, and that no more than three feet, on the whole of the ledge, which was only three or four yards long, and which narrowed to less than two feet in parts. As the rope slackened, Brogan gripped on to the jagged rock face, knowing full well that the worst possible thing he could do was to look down, but he could not help himself and gripped the rock even harder as he felt an almost irresistible urge to jump. He had heard of others who had claimed to have experienced that same urge, but until now he had always dismissed the idea. He would not be so dismissive in the future. He looked up at Jimmy Thompson peering down at him and wondered if there was going to be any future for him, now that he was at the complete mercy of the man who had sworn to kill him. He tried to put such thoughts out of his head as he managed to steady himself and turn his attention to Billy Morgan.

Billy appeared to be unconscious, but with someone like him it was difficult to tell since he always seemed to have a large, toothy grin. The one certainty was that Billy's left leg was broken. The bone of his lower leg protruded grotesquely through a tear in his jeans, the whole leg being buckled under his body, hiding any other possible fractures. A slight movement in the other leg and one arm were the only real indications that he was still alive.

Squatting next to Billy and knowing that his feet were right on the edge and that even a very small shuffle could easily send him hurtling to his death, Brogan somehow managed to pull the unconscious form round slightly, sufficiently to enable him to lift Billy's shoulders and chest and pass a rope round and under. Brogan was very glad that Billy was unconscious. Although he was a dead weight in a very confined space, it was probably much easier than having to cope with the thrashings of an uncoordinated set of arms and legs.

Brogan untied the rope from around his own chest and eventually managed to secure it around Billy's chest and shoulders, looping it around both shoulders and his chest to minimize the possibility of Billy's slipping through while being hauled up. He was eventually satisfied and looked up.

'Take it steady!' he called. 'He's unconscious.' Jimmy Thompson acknowledged that he understood and very slowly the rope began to tighten.

As Billy's body began to slowly rise, it suddenly twisted round and slammed into Brogan's legs and it was only by a lucky grip on a piece of rock that he managed to save himself from falling. The leg which had been broken untwisted itself in a series of sickening cracks and, as Billy cleared the ledge, it hung down almost as if it did not belong to the rest of the body. Thankfully Billy appeared to remain unconscious which made the task of hauling him up a little easier, although great care had to be taken in keeping his head in particular clear of any jutting pieces of rock.

The process of getting Billy to the top took the best part of twenty minutes and when the rope had still not been thrown down to him about ten minutes later, Brogan began to wonder if Jimmy Thompson had decided to leave him there. He was about to call out when the rope suddenly snaked down and Jimmy Thompson looked down and laughed. It was clear that he had thought about leaving Brogan.

When he had secured the rope around his chest, Brogan called up that he was ready and he was suddenly jerked off his feet and he swung out away from the ledge and for a few, seemingly long moments he was allowed to hang, twisting round and round, in mid-air. He heard Jimmy laugh and there was another jerk and he could not help but wince as the rope tightened around his chest, but very slowly he started to rise and was eventually able to control his twisting by gripping the rock face.

His ascent took about the same length of time as Billy's but just as his fingers gripped the top of the cliff, the brothers, on instruction from their father, suddenly stopped pulling and Brogan found himself staring into the hard face of Jimmy Thompson, who had a knife in his hand.

'All I have to do is slice through this rope!' grinned Jimmy, sliding the knife under the rope. 'It's no more'n you deserve, McNally. You murdered my son an' you've done things no man has ever done to a Thompson before in these parts. Give me one good reason why I shouldn't just let you fall?'

'Because it wouldn't prove a thing to

you,' said Brogan. 'Sure, all you have to do is cut that rope, but I think we both know it's not what you really want.'

'And what do I really want?' sneered Jimmy.

'It's not so much what you want,' said Brogan, 'it's what you have to do. You an' me is very much alike, you would've made a very good drifter an' I think the life would've suited you, but you chose the family life. In me you can see the man you might've been an' you have to prove to yourself that you made the right choice all those years ago.'

'Lettin' you fall would prove I made the right choice,' smiled Jimmy, turning the sharp blade of the knife towards the rope. 'You would be dead an' I'd still be alive, that has to be the right choice.'

'It's more'n that an' you know it,' said Brogan. Jimmy nodded and smiled thinly.

'Yeh, I know it,' he conceded. 'I'd

never know who was faster an' more accurate with a gun, but I reckon I could live with not knowin'. You ain't the first saddlebum I've come across, so why should I want to be like you? I sure didn't feel like that with any of the others.'

'Because I'm not your usual type of saddlebum,' said Brogan.

'No, that you ain't, McNally,' agreed Jimmy. 'If you had've been an' you'd murdered my boy, you would've been dead that same day. My other sons wanted to ride into Riverdale that day an' just blast you an' anyone else who got in the way into little pieces.'

'Why did you stop 'em?'

'Because I know better'n they do,' grinned Jimmy. 'I know that they would've been the ones who was blasted into little pieces.'

'Pa!' said one of the brothers. 'We can't hold this darned rope much longer, it's cuttin' our hands. What do we do, just let him drop or pull him up? We is all for lettin' him drop.' Jimmy smiled briefly and removed the knife from under the rope and indicated that they pull Brogan clear.

Although he tried not to show it, it was with a great sense of relief that Brogan unsteadily found his feet and removed the rope. He looked about for Walter and Billy but neither they nor the buckboard were to be seen. Had Jimmy cut the rope or allowed his sons to release it, there would have been no witnesses as to what happened. He also realized what the delay had been in sending the rope back down to him, they were putting Billy on the buckboard and sending it off.

'Where's Billy bein' taken?' asked Brogan. 'Your place?'

'No, there ain't no point,' said Jimmy. 'That leg of his is busted real bad. He needs Doc Graham fast an' the quickest thing to do that is take him straight to town. It'll take maybe three hours on the wagon.'

'Thanks,' said Brogan.

'Don't thank me, McNally,' sneered Jimmy. 'You won't thank me later.'

'I meant thanks for Billy's sake,' said Brogan. 'Most folk in Riverdale seemed to be for lettin' him die out here.'

'I guess even he's got certain rights,' said Jimmy. 'Amos has gone with Walter an' Billy, so there ain't much call for any of us to go into town. I suggest you go, McNally, go while you can, while I'm still in a frame of mind to let you go. Not that I don't intend killin' you, no sir, providin' you is still around tomorrow, which I think you will be, you an' me is goin' to find out just who is the best.'

'And that's important to you?' asked Brogan.

'It wasn't, but it sure is now,' smiled Jimmy. 'If you want to run, I'm givin' you the chance, but somehow I don't think you will. Just like I had the chance just now to finish you off an' didn't take it, I think you have somethin' to prove as well.'

'I might move on,' said Brogan, 'but it sure won't be 'cos I'm runnin' scared, I ain't never run scared yet.'

'I can believe that,' said Jimmy. 'Neither have I, but if you do move on, can you ever be certain in your own mind that it wasn't 'cos you was scared?'

'Chas Brown said that you were a gambler, or had been,' said Brogan. 'I didn't go for that; neither of us are gamblers but facin' you would be a gamble, a gamble for both of us an' the odds are probably about fifty-fifty. I ain't seen you in action, but I have this feel for men like you an' I'd say you was pretty fast. The question you have to ask yourself is—are you fast enough?' Jimmy Thompson shrugged and Brogan mounted his horse and rode off, following the tracks of the buckboard.

TEN

There was a big question mark as to whether or not Billy Morgan would need to have his leg removed, a course of action which Doc Graham did not appear to want to commit himself since, on his own admittance, the biggest thing he had ever amputated in all his years as a doctor had been a man's finger and that had been a good many years previously. As well as the shattered lower leg, the upper leg had also been broken just below the hip and it was this fracture which appeared to be causing the doc the biggest problem. However, for the moment, he repaired both fractures and stitched the wound in the lower leg to the best of his ability and on the face of it he seemed to make a good job of it and splints were applied and stiffly bandaged.

Inevitably, versions of the story of what had happened raced through the town and at each telling acquired new dimensions, particularly the confrontation between Brogan and Jimmy Thompson, usually with Brogan coming out on top but only doing so by trickery in one form or another. The general consensus was still very much that Jimmy Thompson was superior in almost every way to the saddletramp. It seemed common knowledge that both men had had a bitter hand-to-hand fight on the cliff top and that Brogan's draw, this time luckily faster than Jimmy's had eventually won the day. The general opinion was that had it been a fair fight Jimmy Thompson would have easily beaten the saddletramp. But, of course, Brogan had won because all saddletramps were devious liars and cheats.

Whilst Brogan and Walter had been looking for Billy, Mary Tranter had left Riverdale with the documents found in the office and all concerned had succeeded in keeping this fact secret. The story that she was looking for some new clothes for her impending wedding to Barry Day appeared to have been accepted as perfectly natural.

Chas Brown had appeared surprised when Brogan had ridden into town accompanying the wagon with Billy and he had confessed to Barry Day that he had expected the saddletramp to have been killed by Jimmy Thompson and he simply could not understand why he had been allowed to live. He even seemed disappointed that Brogan was still alive.

There was not much more that Brogan could do either for Riverdale or the sheriff. All that was needed as far as Barry Day was concerned was practice and Brogan was quite convinced that provided the sheriff did adhere to a fairly strict regime of learning how to draw fast and shoot straight, he would soon become reasonably proficient and able to hold his own even against someone like Jimmy Thompson.

Knowing that there was nothing more to keep him in Riverdale was one thing, the actual decision to leave was another. Common sense told Brogan that he ought to get out of the place as quickly as possible and to this end he collected the few dollars he had coming to him for his services just in case he did decide to leave suddenly. However, common sense and Brogan McNally were rare bedfellows and Jimmy Thompson had been quite right when he had said that Brogan would not leave until things had been settled between the two since it had become something very deep and personal between them, and it had gone beyond the fact that Brogan had killed Jimmy's son, Frank. In fact, Brogan had heard that Jimmy had said that Frank had been stupid and that it was his own fault, but that was apparently in private; in public Brogan was still a murderer as far as he was concerned.

The remainder of that day, Sunday, passed without incident and by the end of it

Brogan was beginning to wonder if Jimmy Thompson would ever come into town and even started to wonder if Jimmy was really hoping that he would simply leave and he could, thereby, save face. If that had been his thought then he had reckoned without Brogan's own pride or—as some would say—his bullheadedness, but Brogan did not really believe that Jimmy had even entertained such thoughts. He knew that sooner or later Jimmy Thompson would show up.

There were a couple of false alarms when someone had rushed to either the saloon or the sheriff's office declaring that the Thompsons were heading for town in force but when nobody had appeared by about eight o'clock in the evening, both Brogan and the sheriff doubted if they would make an appearance that night.

Having time to think during the evening, Brogan had decided that he would give Jimmy Thompson until noon the following day to show himself and if he had not, he,

Brogan, would definitely be on his way, pride or no pride.

Just after first light found Brogan sitting in Madge's Eatin'-House appreciating the large serving of ham and three eggs she had placed before him and for which she refused to charge.

'Whatever happens,' she said, 'I know this is goin' to be the last meal you eat here. You'll either be ridin' out of town on your horse or ridin' down to the cemetery in a wooden box, so you can have this one on me.'

'I suppose it's all round the town,' said Brogan. 'I'm always amazed at the way things get about when nobody has said anythin'. It's a wonder someone hasn't been out sellin' tickets.'

'Only 'cos they ain't thought about it,' laughed Madge.

'So what's the general opinion about the outcome?' he asked.

'Most folk favour Jimmy Thompson,'

she replied. 'About a quarter think you'll come out on top an' about the same think that for one reason or another nothin' will happen. They say that the most likely thing is for you to get cold feet an' get the hell out of it while you can.'

'And what do you think?'

'Does it matter?' she shrugged. 'All I can say is that if I'd been in your place I would've left town long ago.'

'If I had any sense at all, that's just what I would've done,' he admitted. 'The trouble is I wouldn't know sense if it came an' hit me in the face, but then maybe Billy would've been dead by now.'

'Yeh, I hear that was really somethin'. Did you an' Jimmy really have a fight?'

Brogan smiled and shook his head.

'I didn't think so, Walter says he left with Billy before you'd been pulled up but that you'd never've been able to rescue him if it hadn't been for Jimmy Thompson. Mind, there's some who say it would've been the best that could have happened,' she said. 'Me, I'm not sure what I think. I just wonder what's goin' to happen to him once Silas dies. I can't see Walter wantin' to take him on an' there sure ain't nobody else.'

'I'm goin' round to see how he is when I've finished this,' said Brogan. 'I don't suppose you've heard anythin'?'

'Not a thing, but I did hear last night that he was in a lot of pain,' she said. 'The trouble is I don't suppose he even realizes what happened to him or why he is in such pain.' Brogan nodded and went on to finish his breakfast and then went to see Silas and Billy.

'He's been awake all night,' said Silas, who also appeared to have had little sleep. 'He's asleep now, but how long for his anybody's guess. Doc Graham is comin' to see him again this mornin'. I reckon he'll end up takin' the leg off. Maybe it would've been better to let him die out at Bear Creek Canyon.'

'Is that what you really think?' asked

Brogan. Silas choked back a sob but shook his head. 'Then don't even think about it,' continued Brogan.

'I guess I owe Jimmy a favour too,' said Silas. 'Walter did say that had it not been for his help Billy might never've made it. I know he never had much time for Billy, an' his boys were allus plaguin' him, but it just goes to show you can't allus tell what a feller is really like.' He paused and choked slightly. 'The word is that you an' Jimmy Thompson is headin' for a showdown,' he continued, seeking to change the subject. 'Is that right?'

'So they tell me!' smiled Brogan. 'It seems to me everyone in town knows more about it than I do. I was sayin' to Madge that it's wonder nobody hasn't been sellin' seats an' tickets.'

'They might not have been sellin' tickets,' said Silas, 'but there's been a lot of money changin' hands on the outcome. Jimmy Thompson is on even money, you're on two-to-one with six-to-four on you runnin' out. If you both kill each other all bets are void.'

'I've had worse odds against me,' Brogan laughed. 'Which one of us is your money on?'

'Neither,' replied Silas. 'I ain't no gamblin' man.'

Brogan left Silas and wandered along the street to the sheriff's office where Barry Day appeared to have a problem on his mind.

'I ain't so sure that I ought to allow this thing between you an' Jimmy to happen,' he said. 'It just don't seem right that I should stand by while one of you is killed. The question that keeps comin' to my mind is should I arrest whoever wins an' charge 'em with murder?'

'It'd be self-defence,' Brogan pointed out.

'Would it?' sighed Barry. 'I ain't so sure about that. I know in some countries they allow what they call duellin' an' if someone gets killed that's all fair, it ain't classed as murder, but I ain't so sure if it's allowed here or not. The thing is you're both sayin' that you each intend killin' the other an' if that's the case how can it be classed as self-defence?'

'That's just one of the problems you have to face up to bein' a sheriff,' laughed Brogan. 'Personally I wouldn't even try to stop it or think about arrestin' whoever wins. Anyhow, it might not happen. If he hasn't shown up by noon I'm ridin' out no matter what folk think of me.'

Barry sighed and shook his head. 'I have this feelin' that you won't be ridin' out, leastways not until you've killed Jimmy.'

'Or he's killed me,' smiled Brogan.

'Or he's killed you,' nodded Barry. 'You're a strange one, the thought of dyin' don't seem to bother you at all. Does it?'

'Dyin'? Naw!' smiled Brogan. 'Sometimes the manner of dyin' bothers me a bit, but that's about all. We've all got to die sometime an' when your time comes there ain't much you can do about it or how you die, that's the way I look at it.'

'That might be one way,' nodded Barry, 'but it sure ain't mine. I'm terrified at the thought of dyin'.'

'You're not alone,' said Brogan. 'Still, this time it looks like it's goin' to be either me or Jimmy Thompson. I wouldn't even think about chargin' the survivor with anythin', just accept things for what they are.'

The next thing Brogan did was to drift across to the saloon which on any normal Sunday would have been almost empty as wives insisted that their husbands and sons stayed at home for one day of the week at least. On this occasion, however, the impending showdown between Jimmy Thompson and the saddletramp had made most men defy their wives and a few wives had also stayed behind after the Sunday morning service led by Samuel Bennet, the lay preacher and corn merchant whose sermon that morning had been centred on the fight between good and evil, although most folk did not appear to know whether Jimmy Thompson or Brogan McNally was the good one.

There was a brief silence as Brogan entered the saloon but it quickly gave way to an expectant buzz, especially as a few minutes earlier word had reached the saloon that Jimmy Thompson was on his way. This message was passed to Brogan by Mick Fletcher, the bartender and Brogan responded by saying that he had heard that same message several times the previous night. However, he had the feeling that on this occasion it might just be fact. He ordered a beer and settled himself lounging casually on the counter and waited ...

He had to wait about twenty minutes before someone rushed, panting, into the saloon to announce that Jimmy Thompson and his sons had just crossed the bridge and a couple of minutes later the cry went up from someone looking out of the window that the Thompsons had just ridden up. Brogan's hand slipped to his holster and lifted his gun slightly to make it a little looser and easier to draw, but apart from that he apparently took no notice and casually drank his beer.

'Time's up, McNally!' Jimmy Thompson called from outside. 'You had your chance to turn tail an' run.'

Brogan slowly eased himself away from the counter and ambled towards the window, everyone moving aside as he did so. He looked out and saw a semicircle of men in front of the saloon, Jimmy Thompson in the centre with three of his sons on one side of him and two on the other side, all with legs spread slightly and hands poised to grab at their guns.

'Now them's the kind of odds I like,' called Brogan. 'It's just a pity they're against me not for me. I thought you was a man of principles, Mr Thompson,

I see that I was wrong. I ain't no coward but it would take someone with a brain less than Billy Morgan has got to walk out in front of six guns. Now by my reckonin' there should be seven of you altogether, what happened to the other one? I know there's one dead an' one badly injured, but that still leaves six, so why are there only five of your boys with you?'

'OK, McNally,' laughed Jimmy, 'So you've shown us all you can count ...'

'Yeh, I can count,' said Brogan. 'An' even I know seven against one ain't the kind of odds no man takes. I'd say number seven was coverin' the back door.'

'All we have to do is come on in there an' you'll be dead within' a minute,' said Jimmy.

'But you won't,' replied Brogan. 'You won't on account of you don't know just how many of your boys, or even yourself, will be the first to die, and you can be quite certain that some of you will. I thought this was between us, you an' me,

Thompson. I thought you was a man of principle, at least I had you down as that. Looks like I was wrong though, it looks like you need your boys to hide behind. Just goes to show how wrong a man can be.'

Most of the people in the saloon were too interested in just what Brogan was going to do to notice the back door open slightly and the barrel of a rifle slowly appear and the few who did were too frightened to say anything. However, Brogan had not missed the faint sound of the latch being lifted and had glanced briefly to his side and seen the barrel of the gun. There was a single shot followed by panic amongst the onlookers who immediately charged through both the front and back doors, eventually leaving only Brogan and Mick Fletcher. A body lay in the open door and Brogan nodded to Mick to take a look. During all that time the circle of men at the front had not moved.

'He's still alive,' said Mick. 'He needs help though.'

'That leaves the six of you out front,' called Brogan. 'It seems the boy you sent round the back couldn't wait. He ain't dead, but he needs attention pretty damned quick. Now, Thompson, I'm quite willin' to settle this thing once and for all, but not against six of you. You tell your boys to give up their guns an' then it'll be just you an' me. I could, of course, shoot another one of them now, or maybe even you, but I reckon it'll hurt more if I kill one or two of your sons before I kill you. Which is it to be, Thompson?'

'I'll tell 'em not to do anythin',' said Thompson. 'They stand to one side.' He nodded at his sons who slowly backed back, their hands still poised over their guns.

'Not good enough,' said Brogan. 'That way I reckon I die no matter if I kill you or not. They hand over their guns to the sheriff.'

'You have my word they won't do nothin',' called Jimmy.

'I might have your word, but do I have theirs?' responded Brogan. 'Sorry, Mr Thompson, you tell your boys to hand their guns to the sheriff or you'll just have to take the chance on who gets killed. Sheriff!' he called. 'Are you there?' There was confirmation that he was. 'You go take them guns off them boys an' then I'll come out, but not before.'

Sheriff Barry Day slowly came into view and held out his hand to the first of the brothers who looked at his father questioningly. After a brief moment, Jimmy nodded and the gun was handed over. A couple of minutes later the sheriff had disarmed all the sons and moved well away from them so that they could not overpower him and take their guns back.

'OK, McNally,' called Jimmy. 'Now it's just you an' me.'

Brogan straightened himself, adjusted his gunbelt, flicked his Colt with his fingers, straightened his hat and made his way towards the doorway where he stood defiantly for a few moments, his eyes fixed on Jimmy Thompson but his ears fixed on anything any of the sons might try to do. He had not missed the fact that at least two of them also carried knives.

He stepped slowly across the boardwalk, smiling slightly as he saw the crowd also move a few steps backwards. Jimmy Thompson too, started to back away towards the centre of the street and Brogan stepped off the boardwalk and, slowly, he too moved to the centre of the street.

For a while both men moved either backwards or sideways, their hands poised ready to draw, circling, waiting and watching for the best possible moment, neither apparently prepared to make the first move. Certainly Brogan was not prepared to draw first, not because he was worried that Jimmy Thompson would outdraw him, anything but, in fact he was probably a little too sure of himself, which was why he wanted Thompson to make the first move. It was his way of assuring himself that he would kill his opponent in self-defence.

Even the crowd appeared to be getting a little restless and there were a couple of calls for them to get on with it.

Brogan turned slightly, Jimmy Thompson made his move, Brogan went down on one knee and there were two shots ...

Very gradually and very painfully, Brogan managed to bring his eyes into focus but it was some time before he realized that he was staring up at a wooden ceiling. He thought he called out—at least his brain called out but he was uncertain if the message had ever reached his mouth. However, after what seemed an eternity, there was movement to his side and suddenly a slightly blurred face was peering down at him. When the face eventually managed to get itself sorted out and bring itself into focus, he realized that he was looking up into the chubby features of Madge.

'What happened?' he croaked.

'Jimmy Thompson is what happened,' said Madge. 'The only thing that saved your life was you droppin' on one knee. I was watchin' the whole thing.'

Brogan reached up and felt a bandage around his head and then let his fingers wander down the rest of his body but he could not find any other bandages. What he did find and smell struck more fear in him than any number of bullet wounds would have done. He appeared to be wearing a nightshirt and there was a distinct soapy smell about.

'Couldn't resist it, could you?' he grumbled.

'Resist what?' she smiled.

'Givin' me a bath!' he growled.

'It wasn't exactly a bath,' she grinned, 'more an overall wash. You needed it. I wasn't goin' to let no man in your state dirty any of my beds.'

'All-over wash is the same thing,' he growled again. 'I didn't ask to be put in your bed.'

'You wasn't in no condition to ask anybody anythin',' she said. 'You'll be all right in a day or two.'

'A day or two!' he exclaimed. He struggled to get up but was forced to admit defeat and sank back, his head pounding in protest. 'Jimmy Thompson, what happened to Jimmy Thompson?'

'He's worse'n you are,' said Madge. 'All you got was a creased skull, he took your bullet in his chest. It's touch an' go if he survives or not.'

'I hope he survives,' he said. 'I didn't really want to kill him.'

'I have the feelin' that he didn't really want to kill you either,' she smiled. 'I don't know why the pair of you just couldn't accept things.'

Two days later, Mary Tranter returned to Riverdale with the news that the documents she had handed in were some which had been searched for in the past but never found but now that they had been, investigations would be reopened into alleged fraudulent land and property deals involving certain prominent members of Riverdale. She was never told who those prominent members were, but it appeared obvious that Chas Brown, the mayor, was a leading figure.

That same day, Brogan had pronounced himself fit to travel and had left town before Mary arrived. On the way he called at the Thompson farm where he was met by two surly-faced brothers who at first refused to allow the saddletramp to see their father. It was the intervention of Mother Thompson who said that Jimmy wanted to see him if he was still alive.

'I guess we never really resolved a thing,' grinned Jimmy, weakly. 'Doc says I'm over the worst an' should be OK in a week or two. They tell me I creased your skull.'

'It felt like the top of my head had been blown off,' admitted Brogan, ruefully stroking the bandage still around his head. 'I guess you're right, we never proved nothin'. I didn't hold nothin' back though, as far as I was concerned I was shootin' to kill.'

'Me too!' grinned Jimmy. 'I guess we just put that one down as a draw. If ever you're passin' this way again, call in, maybe we can try again.'

'Thanks, I might just do that,' said Brogan. 'I don't reckon I will though, it ain't often I get to see any place twice. I'll tell you one thing, if nothin' else I reckon I just found out I ain't gettin' no younger. Maybe I should settle down.'

'The only way you'll settle is in a hole in the ground or bein' buzzard meat,' said Jimmy. 'Give my regards to the buzzards!'

The publishers hope that this book has given you enjoyable reading. Large Print Books are especially designed to be as easy to see and hold as possible. If you wish a complete list of our books, please ask at your local library or write directly to: Dales Large Print Books, Long Preston, North Yorkshire, BD23 4ND, England.

This Large Print Book for the Partially sighted, who cannot read normal print, is published under the auspices of

THE ULVERSCROFT FOUNDATION

THE ULVERSCROFT FOUNDATION

. . . we hope that you have enjoyed this Large Print Book. Please think for a moment about those people who have worse eyesight problems than you . . . and are unable to even read or enjoy Large Print, without great difficulty.

You can help them by sending a donation, large or small to:

**The Ulverscroft Foundation,
1, The Green, Bradgate Road,
Anstey, Leicestershire, LE7 7FU,
England.**

or request a copy of our brochure for more details.

The Foundation will use all your help to assist those people who are handicapped by various sight problems and need special attention.

Thank you very much for your help.